LYRIC OF WIND

THE WILDSONG SERIES
BOOK 4

TRICIA O'MALLEY

LOVEWRITE PUBLISHING

"When life takes the wind out of your sails, it is to test you at the oars."

   – Robert Breault

The Fae Realm

Danula

The Light Fae ruled by the Goddess Danu

The Elemental Fae

The Royal Fae Court of the Danula oversee
the Elemental Fae

Water Fae

Earth Fae   Fire Fae

Air Fae

Domnua

The Dark Fae ruled by Goddess Domnu

1

KELLEN

"You have to come down at some point," Alistair, Kellen's best friend and second-in-command, called to him from where they raced their steeds on the wind. As Air Fae, they commanded the skies, and Alicorns were their chariots of choice. Winged unicorns, both fierce and loyal, the Alicorns loved nothing more than to stretch their wings in a good race.

"Make me," Kellen challenged, urging his beast on. He laughed as the Alicorn dove, catching the wind, dipping among the clouds. Kellen's heart soared, as he was always at his most free when he was riding the wind, and not stuck in the royal court dealing with the minutiae of day-to-day royal duties that his father insisted he handle.

Even though he'd stepped into power as leader of the Air Fae over a year ago, his father, Devlin, acted as though *he'd* been the one chosen for the role instead of

Kellen. Once Kellen had been instated, Devlin had shoul-
dered his way into almost every meeting and decision
that had been thrust upon Kellen, acting as though he
had the right to make choices in matters that didn't
pertain to him. They'd gone many a round about it, and
yet, *still*, his father refused to listen to Kellen's requests
that he stay out of Royal Fae business.

His father's actions were causing ripples of distrust
through the Air Fae, and many were starting to question
the choice of Kellen as ruler. Now, Devlin's latest
campaign–for Kellen to claim his fated mate—had sent
Kellen to the skies to escape.

His fated mate.

Like he didn't have bigger things to worry about?

Kellen was beginning to chafe at the responsibilities
that came with being a leader. Each day ended with a
headache from one problem or another, and Kellen was
starting to believe that maybe the people were right.
Maybe he wasn't suited to being their ruler. His father
certainly seemed to think so.

And now his father called for him to find his fated
mate. It was like Devlin just wanted to heap one more
problem on top of his already growing pile of issues to
deal with. Was the man trying to test his limits?

Or was he just jealous?

Kellen's thoughts froze when Alistair cried out,
blood blooming on his chest, and tumbled from the
back of his steed. Kellen dove, urging his Alicorn on,
and still he wasn't sure he'd make it before Alistair hit
the ground. He didn't chance looking over his shoulder
at what had dared enter their sacred space and attack. If

he broke his focus for even half a second, Alistair would be gone.

As the ground screamed toward them, Kellen closed his eyes and pulled at his magick, whispering an incantation that he prayed would save his friend in time. The clouds grew thicker, obscuring his view, and Kellen's stomach twisted as he lost sight of Alistair.

It had been stupid, really, to race into the night, working off his frustrations in the quiet darkness. Alistair, seeing his distress, had reluctantly joined Kellen for a race through the clouds, knowing he'd needed the release. And now, Kellen's decision might cost his friend his life.

Kellen cleared the clouds and issued a sharp command to his Alicorn as they neared the ground at an unsafe speed. The Alicorn, already pulling up, followed Kellen's direction instantly, and Kellen paused for two seconds to assess the situation before slipping his hand from the Alicorn's bridle.

Alistair's body lay on a street corner that was blessedly quiet at this time of night. A woman crouched over him, a guitar on her back and an open case on the pavement next to her. Reaching his hand in the air, Kellen flicked a bubble of protection around the three of them, hiding this scene from the outside world, and dropped from the Alicorn to run to where Alistair lay slumped on the ground.

"Don't touch him," Kellen commanded, his voice sharp, and the woman turned, fear in her stormy grey eyes. Fear was quickly replaced by anger, and she straightened, brandishing her fists.

"I was just seeing if I could help him."

Kellen was too focused on his friend to pay much attention to the woman and her attempt to appear threatening with her tiny fists. He stepped forward, and paused when the woman did as well. What was she doing? Couldn't she see his friend was dying?

"Stay back."

To Kellen's shock, he stepped back a foot. Confusion clouded his thoughts. Who *was* this woman? And how did she have the power to push him back with her voice? They stood and studied each other for a moment, precious seconds ticking by as Alistair 's life drained from him.

"Who are you?" the woman demanded.

"I don't have time for your questions. My friend is *dying*." Kellen brushed past, not caring if he angered her or whatever magick she carried. As he bent to Alistair, his friend dissolved into a liquid puddle of purple blood, and the breath left Kellen's body. *He can't be.* Alistair was gone. His best mate, his *brother*, had left this realm. Anger filled him as he straightened and whirled on the woman who had cost him precious seconds with his friend.

"What in the hell just happened?" The woman sprang back, shock on her face, her eyes wide. To an outsider, a man falling from the sky and dissolving into a puddle of liquid purple blood would be more than enough to send someone screaming for the hills. Yet this woman didn't run. Even though fear was plastered across her pretty face, she stood her ground. *Strange.*

Kellen's royal training kicked in, and he turned to assess the neighborhood around them. Though they stood on what was normally a relatively busy street corner in Galway, there were no cars driving past at this time. What was this woman doing out here at this hour? Kellen glanced down at the guitar case open on the ground with a smattering of coins inside and back to the guitar hanging from the woman's shoulder. A minstrel, he realized. She must play for her coin. Based on his assessment, the scene was secure, except for this woman—the sole witness. Which meant he'd need to bring her with him if he had any hope of keeping this quiet. Reaching out, Kellen grabbed her arm. "You'll have to come with me."

"Like hell I will."

Her swift punch to his face snapped his head back. *The hell?* Who *was* this woman?

He held his fist up to his nose, dabbing at the dripping blood, and narrowed his eyes to where the woman stood in a fighting stance.

"That was unnecessary," Kellen said, deeply annoyed with her.

"Step back." The woman held a proper defensive position, protecting her face and her body with her fists, rocking lightly back and forth on her feet as though she was ready to spring again. Kellen noticed that she didn't turn to run though. Instead, she faced the threat, which apparently was him, head-on. Her courage was admirable even if it was an annoyance.

"I can't have you speaking of what you've seen here this night. You'll need to come with me. I don't have time to argue about this. There's danger afoot, and I can't promise that you'll be safe." Kellen kept his tone even, hoping to convince this woman to come with him. He also didn't need her repeating stories of the Fae around Galway, but as time was running out and the royal guard would have followed him, his options were about to be taken from him one way or the other.

"What do you mean danger is afoot? Am I in trouble? What are you? Did you really come from the sky?"

Kellen took a moment to study the woman, taking in her tousled lavender hair, soulful eyes, and leather jacket thrown over a frilly tulle skirt. Combat boots completed the look. She was arresting in a confusing way—both with a come-hither appeal and a back-off attitude—and he wasn't sure which one to listen to.

"I could ask the same of you, darling," Kellen said. He stepped toward the woman once more. Again, her hands came up.

"Back off." Once again, to his surprise, Kellen found himself unable to step forward. Fury roiled. At her. At whomever killed Alistair. At his lack of control in this situation. He didn't have time for this nonsense. If he couldn't force her to come with him, and he wasn't sure he had the time to test whatever powers she held, then he'd need to secure her silence.

"If I leave you here, how do I know that you'll tell no one of what you saw?" Kellen crossed his arms over his chest and waited for her reply. To her credit the woman took a moment to think about it. A smile broke out on her face.

"Two things. Answer a question for me and pay for my silence. I'll be the first to admit that I'm the mercenary sort, and it would be ideal if I didn't have to worry about where my next meal was coming from."

Kellen scanned the woman's body, for the first time noticing the leather jacket concealed her thin frame. There wasn't much she could do about the hollows at her cheeks. Perhaps she wasn't a very good minstrel.

"What is your question?" Kellen asked.

"What are you?"

"Give me your name," Kellen countered, rocking back on his heels.

"Raven." The woman also crossed her arms over her chest, mirroring his stance, and waited. Time was of the essence now. It was likely his people were at war in the skies above him and now that Alistair was gone, he needed to get moving. "I am Kellen, Ruler of the Air Fae." Kellen wasn't sure why he'd given Raven his name or why he felt the need to let her know his position, however, there was something about her that made him want to prove himself. Which was such an unusual and uncomfortable thought, and he immediately regretted giving her his name.

"Fae," Raven whispered. Instead of fear drifting through her eyes as Kellen often found when humans discovered the Fae, excitement bloomed as though he'd answered a question she'd long held.

"That's the truth of it." Kellen's eyes scanned the dark shadows of the streets. "You'll need to watch your back. There's danger here. Both Dark and Light Fae. I'm one of the good ones."

Raven huffed out a laugh. "That's what all the guys say."

"Believe what you want, but I'm telling you that I'm on the side of good. I don't know what's happened to my friend, and I don't know if the Dark Fae will be following, which is why I'm warning you to sleep with your eyes open. They'll know we spoke. Meeting *me* is a danger to *you*, and they'll now consider you as an asset in their game. If you won't come with me, then the best I can do is warn you. The choice is yours." It wasn't in Kellen's nature to force people to do things, and if she wanted to open herself up to danger, that was on her. "What are your powers, Raven?"

Raven's stormy grey eyes widened.

"My power is my voice." Raven tapped her finger on the guitar that was still slung across her body. "I love singing, and it's not just my job, it's my life."

Kellen noted that she didn't really answer the question, but he was out of time as he heard the winged Alicorns approach in the night. Opening his palm, he showcased a few gold coins which were far more valuable in the human realm than they were in the fairy world. "I have your silence?" Kellen waited for Raven's nod of agreement. When she gave it, he flipped the coins into her case and darted forward, grabbing her chin in his hand, and lifting her face to his. For a moment fear flitted through those gorgeous eyes of hers. "I'll hold you to that."

For a brief instant, Kellen brushed his thumb across the softness of her lower lip, a shock of recognition warming his blood, the spark mirrored in her eyes. And then he dropped his hand, dancing backward before she could punch him again, and hopped on the Alicorn that materialized out of thin air.

"What the..." Raven gasped in surprise. Kellen took to the skies, leaving her alone on the street corner far below, his royal guards circling him. Flying close to one of his most trusted guards, he leaned over, and commanded the guard's attention.

"Stay here with her. Something's wrong. I don't want to lose track of the woman. Keep her safe. Understood?"

The guard nodded, peeling off from the group, and returned toward Galway as Kellen urged his Alicorn on.

Kellen told himself it was because he was worried for her safety as the Dark Fae were ruthless in destroying anyone they thought connected to the good Fae. But it was more than that. Raven of the mournful eyes and tough attitude had enchanted him far more than any Fae woman he'd met before. Maybe, someday, he'd get a chance to investigate why.

2

RAVEN

SHE'D *KNOWN* he was Fae. He wasn't the first she'd seen, though he had a different aura than the others who slipped through the shadows in the early morning hours. Raven wondered if the slightly purplish hue that clung to the Ruler of the Air Fae was the color of the good guys and if the silver men that she'd seen slipping through back alleyways late in the night were those of the "bad" Fae.

Raven slipped a hand into the pocket of her leather jacket, cupping her palm around a gold coin she'd taken from the fallen Fae before Kellen the Ruler had appeared. She wasn't sure what had made her do it, whether it was curiosity or if it was years of living on the streets that made her take advantage of the situation, but she'd palmed the coin and had it in her pocket seconds before the Ruler had hit the ground. Now she pulled it out briefly and studied it, surprised at how the gold warmed to her touch. It was almost as if the coin had its own pulse, which was a creepy thought in its own right. There was a unique design across the front of the coin, a Celtic knot with an etched unicorn in the middle, or in this case, Raven supposed it was the beast that Kellen had flown away on. And just how cool was that? If she'd known that he was going to take her away on a flying unicorn, she might have reconsidered her position on going with him.

Nevertheless, if what the Ruler, *Kellen*, she reminded herself, said was true, then she needed to get moving. One thing Raven had learned in all her years on the streets was to heed warnings from people who were in the know, and was there anybody more in the know on mystical comings and goings than a Fae ruler himself? Bending over, she grabbed the few coins from her guitar case, zipped them into her small wallet, and put the guitar neatly in its case. In moments, she was striding down the empty streets of Galway, chin in the air, eyes ever vigilant. Over the years, Raven had learned how to carry herself, and she no longer feared the night or the empty streets the way most people would. Instead, at some point in her life she'd become one of the night walkers, a term she affectionately used to refer to everyone from the street buskers to the homeless who begged for change on the corner. They were all in the same game, weren't they? Hustling for a living. Just some people were better at it. A light flipped on in a flat, and Raven's stomach twisted as a young mother came to the window, rocking her baby in her arms. Must be nice, Raven sneered, annoyed at herself for being jealous of an infant. She couldn't remember the last time she'd been, or had allowed herself to be, held.

Her boots echoed on the pavement, the quiet of the city settling around her shoulders. Well, as quiet as a city could be. Raven always took extra care to *really* listen, as it could be the difference between being jumped for what change she had made that night, and her next meal. A few drunk voices caught in an argument drifted by on the wind, but not close enough to be a nuisance to her. She turned the corner to her street, grateful to almost be home.

For the first time in her life, Raven had a small spot she could tentatively call home. Granted, it was a month-to-month lease, eviction a constant threat, but nevertheless it was hers. A place to hang her hat, if she had a hat, that was.

"They're stalking you." The man who sat on the dirty pavement near her building cackled as she approached.

"Who is stalking me?" Raven crouched in front of the laughing man. "Come on, Buzz. You can't just be saying that and not give me more information. Who's stalking me?" Raven knew that Buzz largely lived in a sea of his own delusions. However, that didn't mean he didn't see what happened on the streets. Raven tried to make sure he was fed when she could, and warm in the winter. Just because he'd been dealt a bad hand didn't mean he deserved her indifference.

"Raven!" Buzz gripped her arm, his rheumy eyes lighting when he saw her. "There's a pretty girl."

"Are you flirting with me again, Buzz?" Raven smiled,

even though tension knotted her shoulders. "Come on, Buzz. Who's stalking me? You see everything."

"It's the silver men. They're slippery." Buzz made a whooshing sound, dancing his fingers through the air. "They get through the cracks in the street. Jump out of puddles. It's mental, man. Just mental."

"Have they spoken to you, Buzz?" Raven asked. But Buzz had drifted away, lost in his own mind once again, laughing and humming a jaunty tune to himself. Raven squeezed his shoulder and slipped past him, the notes of the song he hummed tumbling around in her head. Music came to her as easily as breathing, and it wasn't a lack of ideas that slowed her down from writing songs. If anything, it was the songs that kept her up most nights, relentlessly dancing through her head, which was why, more often than not, she took to the streets to sing for her supper. She'd made quite a name for herself among the Galway street buskers, and it was because of this that she could afford the little studio flat she now called home. Raven unlocked the outer door of the building, annoyed that the landlord still hadn't put a secure deadbolt on the door, and scampered down the ground-level hallway. Dimly lit, smelling faintly of piss and curry, the hallway was anything but inviting. Glancing over her shoulder, she made sure she was alone before she tackled the locks on her door. Here, she'd spent some of her precious earnings to secure her flat.

It wasn't even that she had much in the way of valuables that had caused Raven to add the extra protection to her door. Due to the necessity of being hypervigilant on the streets, Raven wanted one place she could let her guard down. It was exhausting to always be watching her back, and securing this studio apartment had given her some of the first peaceful nights, well, mornings, of sleep she'd had in her life.

A soft glow greeted her when she slid inside the apartment, carefully locking the door behind her, and Raven let out a sigh of relief. Despite the cost, Raven always left a small LED lamp on in her studio, because she didn't like walking into a dark space. The flat was nothing more than a glorified storage closet, with a sliver of window, and just enough room to fit a daybed. A singular chest of drawers was next to the daybed with a stack of books on top. The kitchen, or what passed for a kitchen, held two cabinets, with a small counter for the kettle and a hot plate. Next to it was a curtain that hid the tiniest bathroom she'd ever seen in her life. Raven kept it scrupulously clean. It was hers, and that was all that mattered.

Taking the guitar off her back, Raven carefully placed it on the stand next to her bed and plopped down to work at the laces of her boots. Before she could take them off, she paused. She had been warned about danger. Would it make sense to take her shoes off if she needed to run? Indecision warred, and then she sighed. Best to be prepared. Leaving the boots on, Raven stood and lifted her mattress. Beneath it was a wood plank that was part of the mechanism that allowed the mattress to fold from flat to sitting, and Raven slid that piece of wood out. It wasn't the most ingenious of hiding places, but it was what she had. Pulling out a wooden box, Raven opened it to reveal three switchblades of varying sizes, a pair of brass knuckles that had been dropped in a street fight, and the one item she'd had since birth. At least she thought it must be from birth, because it had always been with her. A necklace, but not just any necklace. *This* necklace had an intricate pattern on the pendant with words in another language on the back. Despite all of Raven's attempts to discover the meaning, the closest she could discover was that it was from the Fae. How it had come to be in her possession or why she still carried it, Raven couldn't say. For some reason, the necklace was ... *attached* to her and even in the past when punks had beaten her up, stolen it from around her neck, the necklace had *always* found its way back to her. It was a pattern that kept happening, until Raven was half convinced she was losing her mind. One time, in a fit of rebellious youth and fury at not knowing who her family was, Raven had tossed the necklace off a bridge. To her utter dismay, as well as a modicum of relief, the necklace had appeared in her pocket the next morning.

It was the first time Raven had considered that she herself might not also be fully of this world. That same night, she'd taken to the streets to sing. It was on those same streets where she'd then learned her deepest secret and what also might be her greatest power.

"Raven. The silver men are coming." Raven jumped up as Buzz's voice filtered through the thin pane of glass at the window. Raven's blood ran cold. Grabbing everything from the safe, she tucked two blades in her boots, one at her waistband, and threw the necklace over her head. She'd be in trouble if the garda caught her with illegal weapons, but that hardly mattered to her in this moment. For a half second, she debated grabbing her guitar, but it would only slow her down. Instead, she grabbed a pack, tossing in the money she'd hidden under the toilet, alongside the brass knuckles, and hit the hallway at a dead run.

Raven made it two steps into the street before an arm closed around her neck.

3

KELLEN

THE RAYS of the early morning sun danced among the clouds, lighting upon the craggy cliffs where the Air Fae's castle was lodged. High in the sky, the cliffs were unattached to land, and undetectable to humans. Their location made them the trickiest of the Elemental Fae to discover, as well as attack, which was why Kellen was particularly upset about what had just transpired. Not only had he lost Alistair, but they'd been ambushed unawares. It wasn't a good look for him, as a ruler, particularly one whose ability to lead was already in question.

It wasn't that he didn't have the skills to be a leader. Kellen was a confident sort by nature, which was what was needed when flying Alicorns, and he had no issue with giving commands. Instead, a large part of his people's distrust seemed to stem from how his father continued to question every decision Kellen made. If his own father couldn't trust his choices, then how could his people?

Kellen dismounted with a whispered word of praise in his mount's ear, before handing the Alicorn off to a royal guard to see to his care.

"Kellen! Where the hell have you been?" Devlin stormed through the front arches of the castle walls. "We're under attack, and you're out playing with your Alicorns? What kind of leader deserts his people in the middle of battle?"

His father sported a swollen eye and a split lip, and a ripple of pleasure went through Kellen at the sight. Maybe that was a sign of how far their relationship had deteriorated, or perhaps it was just the nature of men and their fathers, but Kellen fleetingly wished he'd been around to see his father take a punch. Naturally, he'd have fought for Devlin, but he'd be lying if he said there hadn't been a time or two over the past year where he'd nearly come to blows with the man himself. It wasn't like Devlin had ever been supportive of Kellen, instead choosing to pit himself as Kellen's greatest critic, under the guise of pushing his son to be the best. He'd become a champion in biting his tongue, but Kellen's patience had grown thin.

Fury bloomed.

"Where was *I*?" Kellen went head-to-head with Devlin, standing a few inches taller than his father, and grabbed the front of his tunic. Devlin's eyes widened, and for a moment, Kellen enjoyed the fear that flitted through his father's eyes. "I was trying to save Alistair. My best friend. My brother. We...he's gone. We've lost him."

A wail went up from behind him, as the Air Fae had gathered to watch the spectacle, and Kellen hated that this was how the news would be delivered to Alistair's family.

"Good riddance." Devlin yanked himself from Kellen's grasp and spat on the ground. Kellen froze. Had his father lost his mind? Alistair had been like a second son to him, as much as he'd been a brother to Kellen. A ripple of unease went through the gathering crowd, and Kellen lifted his chin.

"You dare to speak of our fallen brethren in such a manner? Alistair was family." Kellen gritted his teeth, forcing down the sadness that threatened to overtake him.

"He *was* family. Now he's a traitor," Devlin hissed, and the crowd reacted.

"How dare you?" Alistair's father stepped forward, the light of war in his eyes, his hand at the bow strung to his back. "My son is dead. You'll not speak ill of him." Grief was evident beneath the rage that clung to the man's face.

"I intercepted him trying to steal our amulet. Our most precious possession. Alistair was working for the Domnua all along. How do you think I got hurt?" Devlin pointed to his face, derision in his voice. "Unfortunately, I was unable to stop him, and I fear the Domnua now have our amulet."

A collective gasp went through the crowd, and one woman cried out in distress. Kellen kept his face a mask, his eyes darting among his people, as he tried to process this new information and decide how to proceed. His mind flashed back to Alistair, at the stables with him, moments before Kellen had jumped on his Alicorn and disappeared into the night.

"Kellen...you can't fly right now. I have to talk to you."

"I have to get out of here, Alistair. My father is on me again. Constantly harassing me about one thing or another. I can't breathe. I just need to fly it out, and then I'll be able to think straight." Kellen had hopped on his mount, casting a quick glance at Alistair. *"Come on then. You'll not have me fly alone, will you?"*

"Kellen. There's something you need to know..." Worry had crossed Alistair's face as he'd mounted his own Alicorn. The stable still teemed with people, even at this time of night, the royal guard in constant attendance to the Alicorns and their needs. It was a delicate relationship the Air Fae had with the Alicorns, as they didn't technically belong to the Fae. The Alicorns were free to come and go as they pleased, enjoying grooming, food, and attention in the stables, in exchange for their services in transport. Because of this, there were always people in the stables seeing to the Alicorns. People that could now overhear whatever had brought that look of worry to Alistair's face.

"We'll talk about it out there," Kellen promised. He nudged his mount on, taking to the wind. They'd raced away from the castle, diving among the clouds. *"Sometimes it feels like I just want to fly forever."*

"You have to come down at some point."

They had been Alistair's last words to him before he'd fallen from the sky. Now, Kellen could kick himself for not listening to his friend. Had Alistair wanted to confess to him?

"You're certain the amulet is gone?" Kellen spoke,

focusing on his father. Each of the Elemental Fae had a ruling amulet that gave the leader extra power to guide his people. The loss of it would be catastrophic.

"It's gone," Devlin confirmed, and the crowd shifted, unsure what that meant. Kellen understood their unease. While he was still technically their leader, without the amulet, his powers were diminished. *Was that how Raven had been able to push him back with her magick?*

"We'll recover it. In the meantime, consider our city to be under siege. Enact all safety protocols for war." His people snapped to attention at his command, and the guard began ushering everyone back inside the castle walls. "Once I've spoken with the guard and gathered more details, I will announce a meeting in the great hall."

Relief passed across more than one face, and a few of his people gave him tentative nods of approval. One thing Kellen believed in as a ruler was transparency, which was an area that seemed to particularly grate on his father. However, Kellen insisted on holding bimonthly meetings with his people, making sure to hear grievances and, well, really anything they needed to discuss. It could be tedious at times, but the meetings had gone a long way toward shoring up their foundation of trust that his father seemed bent on dismantling.

If he continued to lead, he would need to address the problem that Devlin had become. He'd known it for a while now and had put it off out of respect for his departed mother, but now they had bigger problems to worry about.

Kellen ignored his father, and with two guards at their back, proceeded inside to the inner chamber where he always secured the amulet before flying. Most rulers would always keep the amulet with them, but due to the precarious nature of flying, Kellen had considered it safest housed in the castle. Now, he stared at where the golden safe lay open, the amulet missing from its bed of velvet. For something that housed so much power, the amulet itself was a fairly simple item. It was a medium-sized gold disc, like a small coin, with an intricate Celtic design showcasing an Alicorn on the front.

"What happened?" Kellen asked his father, staring at the empty safe while his mind whirled. It should have been impossible for the Dark Fae to infiltrate this far into the castle. At least not without assistance.

"I heard a noise. I investigated and found Alistair with his hand in the safe, several Domnua with him. I fought, but they overpowered me and knocked me out. When I came to, they were gone."

Kellen looked around the room. An ornate chamber, it held many valuable art pieces, tapestries, and objects of magick. Something flickered in his gut as he turned in a circle to look at the room.

"There doesn't seem to be much sign of a struggle. How do you think they got in?" Kellen's eyes landed on his father's.

"I put the room to rights myself. It was too distressing to see your mother's favorite salon destroyed by the Domnua. It took heavy magick, but I was able to repair most of it." Devlin's voice was flat, as were his eyes, and Kellen turned away at the mention of his mother.

He missed her.

The queen had been the embodiment of the Air Fae,

light and mercurial, dancing through the air with a lilting singsong quality to her personality. She'd brought joy wherever she'd gone and was dearly mourned by all.

"And how did they breach our walls?" The Domnua were Goddess Domnu's army, the Dark Fae, and while not always the brightest, they were certainly lethal. They killed without a second thought, woman or child, anything that stood in their way really.

"Alistair, I presume," Devlin said. "I'm sorry to be the bearer of such news, as I know how you felt about him. But it's the only explanation."

Had the Domnua used Alistair and then killed him once they had the amulet? He was no longer needed and therefore dispensable? Fury roiled inside him once more, and Kellen clenched his fists.

"It's time to call the others. I'll send a messenger for King Callum."

"The king?" Devlin started forward, grabbing Kellen's arm. "Surely, it's not time to involve the king. How do you think that will look to your people if you have to call for reinforcements already?"

"I think it will look like I know how to collaborate with others in order to ensure the safety of my people." Kellen wrenched his arm away from his father, his thoughts bouncing around his head like a bee trapped in a jar. "Leave me. I must speak with my guard."

Devlin stormed from the room, muttering under his breath, and Kellen stared at the open gold safe, uncertainty churning in his gut.

"How may I assist?" The guard nearest to him bowed his head respectfully.

"Four messengers must ride. This morning. Seek out the others. With our amulet missing, we've become the weak link in the chain, and the opening that Domnu seeks to further her quest for total domination."

"Yes, sir. We'll leave at once." With that, his guard left the room, and Kellen was alone. Crossing to an intricate chest with light blue silk inlaid on the wood, he opened the door and pulled out a small painting of himself with his mother. In it, he was but a little boy, his eyes shining with adoration as he clutched at the queen's skirts. She laughed down at him, delighted with the world in general, and a rush of sadness washed through him. He'd stopped counting the days, the minutes, the hours since she'd been gone. Why bother? In one moment, he could forget she was gone and in the next, it was as though she'd just left him that morning. Grief was tricky like that. It never really went away, and now a new wound had opened with the loss of Alistair. Running a finger over his mother's face, he spoke.

"I vow to protect the people you love. I won't let you down, Mother."

4

RAVEN

RAVEN DIDN'T MIND BEING UNDERESTIMATED. In fact, it often worked to her benefit on the streets. She was thin, due to years of never knowing where her next meal would come from, but that didn't mean she wasn't strong. Or cagey, as she liked to think. She'd even been taught how to leverage her body to use it as a fulcrum to flip people over her shoulder.

That particular move had been learned when she'd been busking on a corner near a jujitsu studio. She'd become so entranced with watching the students through the wide glass window at the front of the training center that the teacher had finally taken notice of her. One day, he'd come out to have a chat as she played. She'd hoped he was coming to drop coins in her case, as she was starving, but instead, he'd surprised her.

"*You seem interested in our classes.*"

"*I am. It's fascinating, actually,*" Raven had admitted. "*You *really throw people around, don't you then? It's funny when the small ones do it to the big guys."*

"You can do it too, you know." The instructor had squinted down at her.

"Maybe." Raven had just shrugged, dismissing the idea. "But I don't have the money for it."

"Would it help you? For your safety?" the instructor had pressed, and Raven had paused in putting her guitar away.

"It would, I'm certain of that. Though I've learned a few moves of my own along the way."

The instructor had cracked a smile at that.

"I don't doubt it. But a little thing like you? You should use all the tools at your disposal. Here's the deal. You keep playing out front, because I like your music, and people stop to listen. When they stop to listen, they see my gym in the back. It's good for business. So, if you keep playing out front, I'll train you. No charge."

"But...but..." Raven looked down at her boots and back at the gym. Most of the students wore expensive exercise clothes or traditional pants with a robe-like top. She couldn't afford that. "I don't have anything to wear."

"Don't worry about it. Plenty of clothes lying about. If you show up, I'll train you."

With that, the instructor had returned to his gym, and Raven had started her training. She'd quickly risen to the top of her class, far exceeding anyone else in her ability to gauge an opponent's next move. She was agile, quick, and cunning—all instincts honed on the streets.

Now, as the arm closed around her throat, Raven's training kicked in. Turning her hip into her assailant, she bent and neatly flipped the man over her shoulder, immediately dancing backward when he hit the ground with a large thud.

"To your right!" Buzz shouted, and Raven pivoted, blade already in hand. Without a second thought, she thrust the blade into the side of the man who launched himself at her, and then gasped when he dissolved into a silvery puddle on the pavement.

"Shite. Aliens!" Buzz crowed as Raven stepped carefully back from the silver puddle of what she presumed was blood. It was much like when the other one, Kellen's friend, had died on the street. Except his blood had been purple. The silver ones had to be the bad guys that the Fae prince had warned her about. Had she been an idiot to ignore him?

A flash of silver was her only warning before another Fae darted at her, but Raven was already kicking her leg out, tripping him as he lunged for her. Without a second thought, she dug the blade between his shoulders as he fell, and he, too, dissolved into a puddle of silvery blood. Her hand shook as she pulled the blade back. *Holy shite. What did she just do?*

She'd never killed before.

While her life had largely been an uneasy and difficult one, Raven had managed to eke out a place for herself on the streets of Galway, connecting to a network of others much like her. For every person that meant her harm, there'd been several more who had her back. It was an unspoken agreement between the night walkers, those relegated to the underground or edges of society. Fringe family, Raven considered them, like a tenuous spiderweb. Easy enough to break, yet surprisingly strong when needed.

A few times, when Raven had found herself in a particularly troubling situation, her fringe family had shown up, helping her out and then fading back into the darkness. Which meant she'd never been forced into drastic measures like the action she'd just taken.

Was it really murder if the person wasn't human?

Those were contemplations for another time, Raven realized, as Buzz shouted a warning. Dancing backward, Raven turned, her stomach plummeting as dozens of silver men poured from the street vents, materializing like genies from their bottles. She raised the arm with the switchblade and dug her hand in her pocket, for a moment forgetting where she'd put her other blades. Heart hammering in her chest, Raven held still while her eyes darted to where the shadowy street corners filled with Fae.

Something warmed to her touch, and belatedly, Raven remembered the medallion she'd taken from the fallen Fae. It sparked under her fingers, as though urging her to use it, and Raven wrapped her hand around the small disc. It seemed to shiver in her palm, warming and pulsing, and a sparkling sort of energy flowed into her. While the medallion was warm in her palm, the energy was cool, like stepping into a waterfall on a hot summer's day. Raven wanted to drink in the power, like her body craved it, and when she refocused on the army of approaching army of Fae, her fear faded away. Instead, Raven lifted her chin and gave the group a lazy smile.

"Hi ya, fellas. Out for a stroll this morning?" Raven said.

"Banphrionsa." A Fae at the front bowed his head, and Raven's eyebrows shot up. What did that mean? Was this a trick? Just moments ago, one of their kind had his arm around her throat, and now another was bowing his head to her? Well, it wasn't going to work. While Raven didn't have extensive knowledge of the Fae, she'd found what she could on her visits to the library through the years. While accounts of the Fae wildly differed, the one thing Raven had learned was that they were tricksters. She certainly wasn't going to view these lads as her buddies now. *Or were they servants?*

"We've come for you, Banphrionsa."

Raven reached for the power she'd discovered years ago, enhanced now by the magickal Fae object in her pocket, and took a deep breath.

"Back the hell up." Her words echoed through the alleyway and bounced off the walls of the quiet buildings lining the street. She needed no microphone, for her power amplified her voice. Relief washed through her when the army of Fae stepped backward. Raven wasn't entirely sure how long she could hold them off, as her power had always been more of a lark to her, and she'd never tested it in such a manner. Frankly, she'd never even confidently *called* it her power before. It was just a weird thing she'd learned she could do.

People responded to what she told them to do. But *only* if she spoke in a certain manner.

At first, Raven had chalked it up to learning about charisma. All day long she watched people. Before, when she'd begged for her food, and after, when she'd played for it, Raven was a watcher. Those who lived on the fringe had to be highly observant. Through the years, Raven became quite adept at reading people—and certain people just exuded power. Some might call it confidence, but to Raven, it was power. It was the ability to walk into a room and command attention, to ask for what they wanted, and get people to listen to them that made these people powerful.

At first, when Raven tried to mimic that charisma, she'd felt silly. But then people started responding to her small requests—simple things, really—and Raven began to test the limits of her newfound confidence. But it was one night, one chilled and damp night, where a group of drunk thugs was harassing a young homeless girl, that Raven had learned her voice might just exceed confidence and dip into something unknown.

The thugs had left, screaming, and the girl had run away from her as well.

But Raven had saved her. So that was all that really mattered.

Not the fact that she'd managed to turn the boys on each other, or that she'd broken one's arm with just her voice. Nope, that wouldn't do well to think too deeply about. So she'd shoved it away for a while, not wanting to uncover what secrets lay deep, because sometimes, well, she'd learned it was best not to pick the scab.

She'd already bled enough, hadn't she? What did it matter where she came from or what made her different? The reality was that Raven lived life on the fringe, and it would likely always be that way.

"Back. Farther. *Leave.* Leave Galway," Raven ordered, focusing on the Fae.

And to her complete shock—*they did.*

In a second, they were gone, the wind whipping a tattered sheet of newspaper across the street where they once stood. *What the hell just happened?*

"Buzz. Are you all right then?" Raven crouched by Buzz, who looked up at her with a gummy smile.

"Aliens. Now I've seen it all." Buzz sighed in contentment, and dropped his head back against the brick wall, sliding into an easy sleep. He didn't appear to be worse for wear, and the Fae hadn't seemed particularly interested in him. No, it was Raven they wanted. But why? *And why had they bowed and called me Banphrionsa?* Glancing once more at the now-empty street, Raven debated what to do. Her instincts told her to keep moving, because if the Fae wanted her for something, it wasn't likely they were going to give up anytime soon. At the same time, they'd responded to her command. Did that mean she could hold them off? For a little while at least? Torn, she made what she hoped wasn't a decision that would cost her her life. Jumping up, she bounded to the door of her building, unlocked it, and ran down the hall to her apartment. In under a minute, she was back outside, her guitar strapped at her back. Sure, she was a touch less mobile with it, but leaving it behind had felt like severing an arm.

The studio was another thing, and Raven glanced woefully at the building, stopping to gently pat Buzz's shoulder.

"Take care, old man." She didn't wake him, for sleep was precious, and instead detoured down the street to her favorite early morning coffee shop where she knew there would be loads of people milling about. There, she'd come up with a plan.

Two cups of steaming black coffee, a sausage roll, and an orange juice later, Raven still hadn't figured out what to do. Part of her kept wishing she'd spoken more with Kellen, as he'd at least warned her of impending danger. She'd had a real Fae speaking to her, and she'd ruined the chance to ask some of her burning questions—most importantly, could he read what was written on her necklace? The pendant hung low between her breasts, a constant reminder that she was different.

Not like she needed that reminder all that often.

"Rough night, Raven?"

"Do I look it then?" Raven glanced up at the tired waitress who'd always been kind to her while she'd counted out her payment most mornings.

"Hair's a bit of a mess."

Which wasn't surprising, considering the racing about that Raven had been doing this morning, but still she shifted and ran a hand over her hair. Dying it lavender had been a bit of fun she'd tried after discovering there were inexpensive dyes that worked easily on her light blonde hair. It had been the one spot of vanity she'd indulged in, next to her used leather jacket and serviceable boots. They were the only jacket and boots she owned, so she'd scrimped and saved until she could afford the best charity shop purchases she could find. It had been worth it, however, because her feet stayed warm, and her jacket provided protection from the elements. The tulle skirt she regularly wore had been marked to almost zero, and she'd grabbed it without a second thought. This outfit had become a uniform of sorts for her, the juxtaposition of hard and soft, and she carefully washed the skirt and hung it to dry every few days.

Nodding her thanks to the waitress, she stopped by the toilet to freshen up, acknowledging that she did, indeed, look a touch wild this morning when she saw herself in the mirror. Her hair stood out in all directions, and dark circles smudged her eyes. She didn't have any makeup, so there wasn't much she could do about the dark circles, but she ran her hands under the tap and smoothed her hair, before dusting dirt off her jacket. After using the toilet, Raven left the diner with a wave goodbye, knowing she needed to keep moving.

Maybe there was a way to summon Kellen back? If so, she might be able to ask him what was going on. She kicked herself for being stubborn and pushing him back, all while feeling very much alone. *Sadly, that wasn't a new feeling for her*. Raven then pushed inside the front door of her favorite place in the world.

The Galway Youth Centre was a space for forgotten kids like she'd been. Children who were in and out of the foster system, children who never knew where they were going to sleep the next night, children who didn't trust easily. Raven had started volunteering there a few years ago when she'd stumbled across it on an early morning walk home from a night of busking. Now, she went regularly to the Saturday morning group, where she'd teach the kids music or just be a sounding board when they needed to vent. It was pretty incredible what the children would confess, when teasing out a song on the guitar, and Raven did her best to listen and provide encouragement where she could. It wasn't always easy. She lived a hard life. These children likely would as well. Maybe that's why they liked her so much. Raven never sugarcoated anything. She was a realist to the core, so instead of promising them a future that seemed beyond reach, Raven taught them ways to deal with life in the now.

"Raven!" Taryn, one of her favorites, ran over and stopped short of giving her a hug. Physical intimacy was difficult for most of the kids here. Instead, they bumped fists and Raven noticed a light bruise on Taryn's cheek.

"What happened?" Raven asked, nodding to Taryn's cheek as she pulled the guitar off her back and took a chair in the corner. The room was set up with tables and chairs pulled to various areas to create little conversation corners, so the kids could have space while they worked through whatever they needed to work through. It was a safe space for them to just be, even if all they ever did was sit quietly in a corner, like Daniel who never lifted his head from his book.

"I tripped." Taryn grinned at Raven's look. "Really this time. I was trying to get a lady's iPhone back for her."

"Why? Who took it?" Raven handed Taryn the guitar, keeping her eyes on the window in case of any silver men walking by.

"Stupid street rats," Taryn muttered, bending her dirty head to the guitar. Raven's heart twisted. Taryn always tried to differentiate herself from the kids who picked pockets for a living, her heart full and aching for love, and she tried to land on the side of good. There were times when that line blurred, but mostly Taryn was a great kid. Raven wished she could do more for her.

"Did you get it back?" Raven asked, tugging on a lock of Taryn's hair.

"I did."

"Thatta girl. Remember the move I taught you, right?" Raven had also been teaching the kids how to protect themselves, her jujitsu training coming in handy.

"I did. I do."

"Listen, Taryn..." Raven stopped as Taryn's eyes shot to hers, a worried look on her face. Of course, Taryn had already heard the tone of Raven's voice, and as someone attuned to changes in her environment, she already knew what was coming.

"You're leaving." Taryn pushed the guitar into Raven's lap, and stood, ready to run.

"Not by my choice," Raven said, grabbing Taryn's arm before she could run away. "Look at me. *Look* at me, Taryn." Raven stopped short of using her voice power. Finally, the girl looked up at her.

"I don't *want* to leave you. But I think I'm in trouble. And if I bring this trouble here, you might get hurt. This isn't about me wanting to leave you. What did I promise you?"

"Fringe friends forever," Taryn whispered.

"Exactly. Is there any way that I can reach you so that I can tell you I'm safe? Or that once things have settled down, that we can see each other again?"

"Right. You'll be contacting me then? Like that'll happen."

Raven wasn't surprised by Taryn's tone or doubt.

"It will happen, Taryn. I've never lied to you, and I'm not starting now."

"Mmm, I guess. I do have an email address. Sometimes I can check it on the computer here when they let us on. I'm really bad at typing though." Taryn shrugged, her eyes sad.

"Give it to me. I'll email when I can. I promise you, Taryn. Fringe friends forever."

"Okay." Taryn shrugged and rattled off her email. She smiled wistfully, more adult than child, used to life handing her disappointment after disappointment. "Sure, and I'll see you down the road sometime."

"It's not goodbye," Raven promised, but Taryn had already abandoned her, moving to the other side of the room, needing to put her walls up. Raven understood that, as much as it hurt her to see the protective behavior.

This was for the best. Until she knew what was going on, Raven couldn't put these kids in danger. With her heart heavy, she slipped out the back door and took to the streets. Once again, she was alone, the only certainty she'd ever had in her life.

5

KELLEN

KELLEN WENT where he always did when he needed to find peace—the stables. He'd never minded getting dirty and would often throw in next to the guards as they mucked out stalls or groomed the Alicorns. While many of the tasks could be done by magick, Kellen found he enjoyed the physicality of working with the Alicorns and being hands-on with their care.

"A handsome prince you are," Kellen said, stopping when Riker, his favorite Alicorn, nudged him for attention. Kellen wrapped his arm around the Alicorn's neck, bringing his forehead to the side of Riker's head, and the two stood like that for a moment. One of the unique things about Alicorns was that they could communicate in imagery, and now Kellen smiled as Riker projected a pretty waterfall scene into Kellen's mind. Riker clearly sensed that Kellen needed soothing.

"We'll have ourselves a ride out there soon, Riker. I

can't get away at the moment. Listen..." Kellen eased back to meet the Alicorn's friendly gaze. "There's danger just now. The Domnua. I'm sure you well know, after losing Alistair yesterday, but it's important you warn the others. I don't want to lose any of you. It would, just, *kill* me if you were hurt." Kellen's voice cracked, and Riker bumped him with his nose.

Now, an image of Alicorns shooting fire from their horns presented itself in Kellen's mind, and Kellen smiled softly.

"I know you can protect yourselves. But I'd prefer it not to come to that. Next time we fly, though, I want you in protective gear. Tell the others. No Alicorn flies without their shield. Understood?"

Riker stomped his foot once, as though to say he agreed, and Kellen felt marginally better. The Alicorn was a unique and majestic beast, a blend of Pegasus and the unicorn, and their magicks were almost as strong as the Fae's. Stronger, in some areas, Kellen thought.

"Sir? The king has arrived." The guard who stopped at the stall could barely contain his excitement. Kellen couldn't blame him. While Callum's mother had periodically visited each of the Elemental Fae to ensure peace and balance among her people, many hadn't met the new king yet. It had been told that his partner, Lily, had been meant to ascend the throne but had bowed out, instead giving the ruling power over to Callum, as, being human, she still had more to learn about the Fae world. It was a wise decision, and Kellen looked forward to speaking with both Callum and Lily. He hoped the other Elemental leaders would be able to attend as well, but from his understanding, they were staunchly staying by their people's side in this time of turmoil. He could hardly blame them. Kellen could only imagine the guilt he'd feel if the Air Fae were attacked, *again*, while he was gone. Luckily, it seemed it was only his father and Alistair that had been injured in the most recent attack, while the rest of his people remained unharmed.

Grief tugged low in his gut as he thought about Alistair. He truly hated to believe that his friend had been a traitor. It didn't sit well with him, but that was the nature of bad news, wasn't it?

An image of Alistair, smiling and playing with the Alicorns flashed into his mind, along with the word: *friend*.

"Yes, Riker. Friend. He's gone now," Kellen said, and turned, nodding for the guard to escort him from the stables. Riker's image stuck with him, as though the Alicorn was trying to tell him something more, but he was distracted by his father waiting at the entrance.

"You'll tell them about the amulet?" Devlin demanded, brushing an imperceptible wrinkle from his blue tunic piped with metallic gold threading. Devlin liked to dress the part of a royal, and Kellen supposed he couldn't really fault him. The Fae did love a certain level of extravagance.

"I can hardly keep it a secret, can I?" Kellen asked, handing his gloves off and brushing the dust from his shirt before striding from the stables to meet the arrivals.

"You can't meet the king like that," Devlin protested.

"Surely the king won't stand on ceremony if there's a war at hand," Kellen said. Even the smallest of decisions

warranted a critique from his father, and it took everything in Kellen's power not to order the man back while
he met with the king on his own. It wouldn't do to start a
confrontation with his father, not now, when so much
more was at stake.

Had Devlin always been this way, or had it intensified
when Kellen's mother had died? It all blurred a bit, with
the grief of his mother's passing greying the edges of his
memories, but a part of Kellen felt that the intensity of
his father's focus stemmed from Devlin's inability to
grieve the loss of his wife. It seemed he focused on what
he could control, his son, rather than addressing his
emotions. At least that's what Kellen kept telling himself,
as he reached for patience day after day with Devlin.

"Welcome to our home," Kellen boomed, brushing
Devlin aside when he saw the king standing by two
Alicorns and a slew of royal guards. Next to him stood a
slender woman with brown hair, a delighted smile
creasing her delicate face. Though King Callum's face
was cut in hard edges when he surveyed his surroundings, his countenance instantly softened when he looked
down to his wife. At his words, the two turned to him.

"I just can't get over it," Lily gushed, taking the lead,
and stepping forward. His father let out a huff of surprise
at his side, and Kellen was reminded how often Devlin
had chaffed at his mother's leadership. "Flying unicorns.
I mean, they're truly magickal, aren't they?" The Alicorns
shook their manes and stomped their feet, preening
under her attention, and Kellen wondered if Lily knew
that they understood her every word.

"We're lucky to have them as our friends and our

allies," Kellen agreed, holding his hand out to Lily. "Not only are they incredibly powerful, but the Alicorns are a deeply honorable and ancient race. They carry strong magick and a love for flying. It's a uniquely beneficial relationship, and I, for one, have a hard time staying out of the stables myself. It's nice to meet you, Queen Lily. Even under such circumstances. I'm Kellen, leader of the Air Fae, and this is my father, Devlin."

"Kellen. We met once, ages ago. Do you recall? The race at the Solstice Festival?" King Callum stepped forward, his arm automatically going around his wife's shoulders, while he grinned amiably at Kellen. It took Kellen a moment to remember, for he'd been but a boy of ten or eleven at the time, and then he threw his head back and laughed. The Solstice Festival hosted a wide range of magickal competitions and rites for all ages, and Kellen and Callum had challenged each other in a race through the woods that had resulted in Kellen dunking Callum in the river.

"I'd forgotten," Kellen admitted, warmth blooming. "You've dried out, I see?"

"Eventually. My pride still stings." Callum shook his head, mocking embarrassment, and the two men shared a quiet chuckle over days passed.

"What are you two talking about?" Devlin demanded, a harsh edge to his tone, and King Callum shot Kellen's father a questioning look. Kellen was used to it by now, as Devlin inserted himself into everything, but this time he felt compelled to put his father in his place. What they needed now was an alliance with the king that would protect not just the Air Fae, but all of the Elementals. The last thing he needed was to get off on the wrong foot with the king.

"Father, see to the Alicorns please. They've journeyed far with our friends here and will need special attention."

Devlin's mouth dropped open at the dismissal, a flush of red crossing his cheeks, but even he seemed to know when not to push it. With a curt nod, he turned away while Kellen gestured for Callum and Lily to follow him into the castle.

"I have to say, I continue to be astounded by the beauty of the Fae world," Lily said, holding a hand to her chest as they strode through the arches of the castle and wound their way through a side corridor cut into the craggy rocks of the cliffs.

The castle itself was built in a unique fashion. Due to the nature of the magickal cliffs that the Air Fae had chosen as home, the topography didn't allow for one large building in a singular spot. Instead, the main entrance of the castle broke off into an artery of passage-ways, leading to different rooms, wings, and outposts of the castle grounds tucked among the dips and crevices of the cliffs that spired into the sky. It made their castle particularly difficult to infiltrate, as royal guards could monitor the sky from all vantage points, and the labyrinth of tunnels burrowed through the cliffs would lead to confusion for anyone attempting to traverse the passages. Not Kellen, though. He'd grown up running through every tunnel in the kingdom, and soon navigating them had become as second nature to him as flying on the back of an Alicorn.

"We Fae are a fanciful lot, aren't we? It's a flair for the

dramatic we have," Kellen said, pointing at the ceiling of the tunnel where tiny fairy lights were embedded in the rocks. "How are you finding your adjustment to our world?"

"I think I just live in constant surprise and wonder," Lily admitted with a soft laugh. "It's a dream come true, and that's the truth of it. That being said, I understand it's not all fun and fairy tales. I'm...well, I'm nervous for the Fae. I worry about what the future will hold if Domnu gains a foothold. She's ruthless."

The Dark Goddess, Domnu, had systematically been working her way toward stealing the power back from the Elementals, determined that her dark army would rise up and rule both Fae and humans alike. It was no small feat for even a goddess, but it seemed Domnu was closer than ever to achieving her goal. Particularly now that she had their amulet. Kellen dearly hoped that this wouldn't be the thing that shifted the balance in her favor.

"It's right to be wary of her. She'll never give up. Domnu has waited centuries for this and losing the Four Treasures was a crushing blow. Now she wants vengeance. She's growing increasingly unpredictable." Callum ducked his head through the doorway that Kellen indicated, and soon they were ensconced in Kellen's private chamber, the same chamber where the amulet had been stolen. Attendants arrived immediately and set up refreshments on the side table while Lily wandered the room to marvel at the art. Only once they were alone did Kellen speak.

"I have troubling news to share," Kellen said, clearing his throat. He hated having to be the first of the

Elemental leaders to admit that they'd lost their amulet. But there was no way for him to hide the missing treasure from the king. His powers were now diminished, and it could put his people in jeopardy if he didn't ask for extra protection. "Two days ago, the castle was infiltrated while I was on a flight. It was a dual-pronged attack. Both my best friend and my father were caught in harm's way. We lost my friend, Alistair, and while I sought to protect him, my father lost the battle of protecting our amulet. It's missing." Kellen gestured to the empty safe behind them and both Callum and Lily turned to look at it.

"And this is why you called for me?" Callum asked, moving to the sideboard to pour a cup of tea for Lily. Kellen noted that Callum didn't request the service of a servant, instead he saw to Lily's comfort on his own.

"Yes, I'm sorry, but I had no other choice. I fear my people are in danger, and as I'm fairly new to the position, I worry that my reduced powers will not be enough to protect them. My people come first."

"Admirable," Callum said, nodding to Kellen before handing his wife a cup.

"This place doesn't look like there was a battle," Lily observed, her cheeks pinkening when they both looked at her. "Sorry, I shouldn't interrupt."

"Your insight is always welcome, my love. Remember, you outrank me," Callum said, his tone mild, as he ran a finger across her cheek.

"Not really." Lily rolled her eyes. "You're the king. I'm just a human learning the ropes. Anyway, did you magick everything back to rights then?"

"My father says that is the way of it." Kellen poured

his own cup of tea and sat on a green silk armchair across from Lily.

"Convenient, isn't it? Having magick to clean things up?" Lily mused.

"If Domnu has your amulet, the potential she has to control your people grows significantly. Unless your people are very loyal to you." Callum measured Kellen with a look that had him inwardly cringing.

"To my mother, perhaps," Kellen said, squeezing the bridge of his nose with his fingers. "Me? That's a work in progress, I suppose. It's been a difficult transition year. Their queen, my mother, well, she was deeply loved by all."

"Yourself included," Lily said, sympathy lacing her tone.

"Yes, myself included," Kellen said, his shoulders drooping. "I miss her, terribly. And I've done my best to lead in her stead, but it's sorely hard to grieve and be a leader at the same time."

A hand landed on his shoulder, and Kellen glanced up at the king in surprise.

"I understand. You should have come to me with your concerns. We could have commiserated together in our shared grief." Kindness etched King Callum's face, and Kellen was reminded that he, too, had lost his own mother not too long ago.

"I didn't think to bother you with such matters," Kellen said. He looked up as voices sounded in the corridor.

"Fairy light ceilings? How cool is that?" a woman's voice exclaimed. "Look how they're built into the rock. It makes it look like the whole tunnel sparkles."

"Bianca!" Lily put her tea on a small table before jumping up to hug a softly rounded woman who stepped through the door with a lanky man at her back. "It's been ages since I've seen you."

"Well, you know, busy with the whole 'saving the world' thing. Let me look at you," Bianca said, pulling back to study Lily's face. "Love looks good on you, Lily. You're positively blooming."

"Seamus, Bianca. Meet Kellen. He is leader of the Air Fae and there's been a recent attack by the Domnua that has left him without his amulet. The Air Fae's security is now compromised, and we believe that means Domnu is readying for war. The other leaders are shoring up their protection at their homesteads, and we'll need to figure out our next steps here," King Callum said while shaking Seamus's hand.

"Yes, sir!" Bianca snapped her heels together and saluted, and Callum grinned.

"At ease, soldier," Callum commented and despite the severity of the situation, Kellen fought a smile. Whomever these two were, they clearly had a warm working relationship with the king.

After introductions were through, the new arrivals made themselves some tea and then joined Kellen, Lily, and Callum on the couches.

"If your amulet is truly gone, that presents a problem to our plans," Bianca surprised Kellen by taking the lead.

"Which plans?" Lily perked up. "What we found in the book?"

"Correct. I'm human as well." Bianca smiled at Kellen. "So I've had a bit of catching up to do. The good thing is that I love research. Lily and I have been making use of the Fae library at the Danula's castle, and we did find one ritual in particular that might be an option for banishing a Dark Goddess once and for all. Potentially our only viable option, really."

"You found a spell for ridding the world of Domnu?" Kellen's mouth dropped open, and he shifted, reassessing the women. Not only were they kind, but it appeared they both were also whip-smart. "That's incredible. Sure and I've had researchers looking for a while now."

"Right place, right time?" Bianca shrugged cheerfully. "Hard to say. But the spell calls for all four amulets of the Elemental Fae to be sacrificed to the magick. It's...a tall ask, that's the truth of it. One all of the leaders will need to consider seriously."

"And without all four amulets?" Callum asked. Kellen's heart dropped. Hope had bloomed for a moment in his chest, but without his amulet, there might be no reason to pursue this route.

"Hard to say. Perhaps we could mimic an amulet? Put a similar level of power in it?" Bianca said, tapping a finger on her mouth.

"What are our next steps without it?" Kellen asked, turning to the king. There wasn't much that could be done in this moment about his amulet being gone, so he needed to know how else to protect his people.

"We need to prepare for war. She's coming, one way or another."

"I feared as much." Kellen's heart sank. Losing Alistair

had left him with a heavy feeling in his gut the last two days, as though his very soul was sinking beneath the surface of stormy waters, and now he feared his best friend wouldn't be the only loss he endured before this was through.

"Unless we could get Danu here," Bianca added, and they all looked at her. Danu, the Goddess of Light, was Domnu's only sister.

"How so?" Lily asked, stretching her legs out in front of her as she took a sip of her tea.

"Remember that added note? At the bottom of the ritual? About blood of my blood?" Bianca turned to Lily and Lily's face brightened.

"Oh, right! I'd forgotten about that. Yes, it seemed to suggest that the only other way to kill a goddess was with the blood of her own family."

"So we'd just need Danu to prick a few drops of blood and pour it into Domnu's mouth? Poison her?" Kellen raised an eyebrow in surprise.

"Maybe?" Bianca shrugged. "I haven't found anything else that clarifies the meaning of it, but it kind of makes sense. If goddesses are meant to be immortal, then only hugely powerful magick or a ritual made with their own blood can destroy them. I just don't see Danu offering up her blood."

"Even one drop could make the weakest of men an almighty ruler," Callum agreed.

"She'd trust nobody with it, well, if she was smart," Bianca agreed.

"So we need to get Danu to do it herself," Lily suggested.

"Right, so either we find the amulet and convince the other elementals to give up theirs in a united ritual to destroy the Dark Goddess or we get her sister to kill Domnu herself. No problem," Seamus said, and the group laughed despite the intensity of the situation.

"Where do we start?" Lily blinked pretty doe eyes at them, and Kellen understood in that moment just how lonely he was. Callum had gone to sit by Lily, casually leaning into her, while Seamus ranged himself behind Bianca, subconsciously protecting her.

And Kellen sat alone. His mother gone. His best friend murdered. His father an unstable support system.

"Sir?" A guard poked his head in the door, and Kellen stood. Crossing the room, he stepped into the hallway with the guard and closed the door behind him.

"What's the problem?" Kellen knew it must be bad if the guard had dared to interrupt a royal meeting.

"It's the girl. The one you had us watching in Galway? She's in trouble. The Domnua are hunting her. While she's held them off thus far, it's only gotten worse. I wanted to request the ability to intervene if necessary?"

Raven's face sprung to mind, her defiant chin and world-weary eyes, and he felt an irrepressible tug in his heart to go to her.

"It's surprising they are targeting her with such vehemence. I wonder why?" Kellen looked at his guard.

"I, too, wondered the same thing."

"We need to bring her back here. For her safety," Kellen said. It didn't matter that he wanted to see her again. What mattered was the Domnua wanted Raven for some reason, and until they figured out what that was, the woman wasn't safe. "Give me a moment to speak with the others."

"Problem?" Callum asked, both him and Seamus standing at the ready as Kellen returned to the room.

"There's a woman..." Kellen quickly filled them in on his interaction with Raven, and by the time he'd finished, Bianca had also risen and was dusting her palms off on her pants.

"Well, then. Let's go," Bianca said, surprising Kellen.

"Let's go?" Kellen echoed, tilting his head at her in question.

"Surely you don't think this woman is going to come with the likes of you? She'll trust me though. I'm human. And I'm charming. Isn't that right, my love?" Bianca winked at Seamus.

"She can charm a gold pot off a leprechaun," Seamus agreed.

"But...is it safe for you to go with me?" Kellen countered.

"I fear I haven't had a chance to fully bring you up to speed," Callum said, stepping forward. "Bianca and Seamus were integral in the battles of the Four Treasures. They've kindly been of assistance to us since Domnu has returned in her quest to destroy the Danula Fae. There isn't much they haven't seen or fought against. Bianca's right, she's one of the strongest tools at your disposal."

"That's the first time I've enjoyed someone calling me a tool." Bianca grinned as she elbowed the king in the ribs, and Kellen gaped at the overt familiarity before shaking his head to clear the shock away.

"In that case, are you ready to ride again?"

"On an Alicorn? Hell yes, I am!" Bianca shot her fist in the air and grinned, and despite himself, Kellen did as well.

He, too, felt the same every time he mounted an Alicorn.

"Then, by all means, let's fly."

6

RAVEN

SHE NEEDED TO KEEP MOVING.

Keep moving and keep to crowded places, Raven amended, as she wove her way through the main streets of Galway. It was Saturday, a busy shopping day, and Raven hoped if she kept herself surrounded by enough people that she'd stay safe until the evening.

It seemed the silver men preferred the cover of darkness anyway.

They'd visited her once more the night before, and she'd held them off yet again. Not without considerable effort, and now her shoulders drooped as she paused beneath an overhang to get out of the misting rain.

It had been over forty-eight hours since she'd slept.

Raven hadn't returned to her flat, instead slipping through old haunts and crevices in the city, seeking to stay underground as much as she could. Her heart was heavy at leaving Taryn behind, and her flat, but there wasn't much to be done about either of those things. Danger had landed on her doorstep and Raven wasn't one to wish away reality. There was no point in wishing for anything, really, when life served up exactly what it wanted to, *when* it wanted to. They were all subject to the whims of fate, bit players in the game, simple pieces to be moved around on a chessboard. The thought of being out of control rankled at Raven's fierce independent spirit, but she'd dealt with the government enough to know just how little control she had over her own life.

Now, she leaned a shoulder against the damp stone wall of the market and watched the passersby with careful eyes. Mothers hurrying children who just wanted to stomp in the puddles, bike messengers delivering takeout food, and students off class for the weekend rushed past, everyone used to the damp weather. As rain went, it was hardly something to be noted, but still the dampness seemed to soak into Raven's bones. She was tired, that was all. Normally, she wouldn't fuss much about a spot of rain either. But now, all she wanted was her bed, a locked door, and ten hours of uninterrupted sleep.

A luxury she wouldn't be getting anytime soon.

A glimmer of silver shone from a puddle, and Raven straightened, her eyes widening. Was she going crazy or were the silver men really materializing out of the puddles that clung to the damp pavement? She blinked in disbelief as several of the silvery army formed, right in the path of pedestrians, and not a single person glanced their way.

Right, then. Maybe she was finally losing it? Nobody

else seemed overly concerned with the presence of the strange silver men that turned in unison to stalk in her direction. In fact, one mother even towed her determined child *through* one of the creatures. The child howled, looking like it had been slapped in the face, but the mother continued on without another look in Raven's direction. But Raven saw it. The child had *felt* the silver man. It wasn't just her.

Which meant she needed to *run.*

Raven darted around the corner and ducked into an alleyway, hoping to make a sharp left, and come up the other side of the street behind the silver men. But luck was not on her side this day. Not that it ever much was. Skidding to a stop in front of a wall of silvery Fae, Raven held up her hands, whirling as the others flanked her from behind. This was the most she'd had to deal with yet, and her heart thudded in her chest as she tried to summon the courage to use her power.

She was just so damn *tired.*

Maybe it was better to just give in. They weren't going to stop hunting her, it seemed, and if she never got a moment's sleep, then eventually, she'd just collapse, and they would be on her anyway. Surrender wasn't in her nature, but if she went now, with her wits about her, maybe she'd be able to protect herself from serious harm. Her shoulders slumped as she stepped back until the guitar she wore at her back brushed the wall of the alley.

"Why don't you boys tell me what it is you're after? Why me? I'm a nobody," Raven said. The leader opened its mouth to speak, but a flash of light was the only warning they had before magick rained down from above. Raven ducked as bolts of fire darted from the sky, and a flutter of wings and pounding hooves sounded on the pavement. Crouching, she glanced up to see several of the flying Alicorns racing through the alleyway, fire searing from their horns, as the silvery Fae were ruthlessly destroyed. In moments, the alleyway was covered in silver blood that seeped slowly into the pavement before disappearing.

"I bet you wished you'd taken me up on my offer." Kellen smirked at her from where he sat astride the majestic beast. Raven was too in awe of his presence again to make a snide remark back.

She'd forgotten just how beautiful he was.

Strikingly blue eyes, the color of the sky on a perfect summer's day, and jet-black hair made him a commanding presence. But it was more than just his looks–it was the easy confidence in how he handled his Alicorn, his muscular thighs hugging the beast, his lazy smirk a challenge.

Raven was glad she'd punched him.

She shouldn't be. He'd just saved her from the danger, yet how was she to know that he was any less dangerous than the other creatures who had just cornered her?

"Not in the slightest," Raven said, lifting her chin higher, as his Alicorn stomped a hoof in front of her. She really wanted to step forward and pet the beautiful animal. Raven had to force her hand into a fist to stop herself from reaching out. "I had this handled."

"Did you then?" Kellen barked out a laugh. "From the looks of it, you were on the edge of surrendering to the Dark Fae."

"Not at all. I was luring them into complacency," Raven countered.

"And then what? You were going to murder an alley full of Dark Fae? While literally swaying on your own two feet? You wouldn't last a minute in battle," Kellen scoffed.

"Care to try me?" Raven challenged, raising a fist to remind him she'd already gotten one past him before.

"Is this how you convince women to trust you?" Raven turned at the voice to find a smiling blonde woman sliding from her Alicorn with the help of a tall lanky redheaded man. "If so, I fear you're missing the mark."

"Oh, I'm meant to be trusting this one, am I?" Raven laughed and shook her head, keeping her eyes on Kellen's icy-blue ones. "And what reason has he given me to do so?"

"I didn't force you to come with me against your will, did I? Though judging from the looks of it, I should've," Kellen countered.

"Hi." The blonde jutted out a hand, stepping in front of Raven and cutting off her conversation with Kellen. "Ignore him. I'm Bianca, I'm human as well, though I've fallen in with this lot of Fae and have never been the happier for it. This one's mine. Hand's off." Bianca jerked a thumb at the redhead who grinned cheerfully at Raven. She immediately warmed to them.

"Understood," Raven said.

"What this one is doing is a horrible job communicating that we are here to help you, and while it seems super sketchy, it would be great if you could come with us because we've got bigger things to worry about than swooping down here every two seconds to save you. Can't say why the Dark Fae are after you, but this is your chance to come with us so you can be given a reprieve. For the moment at least," Bianca said, tilting her head at Raven. "Sure and you're looking a touch knackered then, aren't you?"

"I'm..." Raven was shocked when her voice cracked. "I'm dead tired, and that's the truth of it."

"Come with us. I'll stay with you while you sleep. If Kellen's your concern, I outrank him. I'll keep him well in his place."

"Like *I'd* hurt a woman," Kellen burst out, fury on his face, and Raven had to admit the truth of his words. He hadn't been the first man she'd punched in her life, but he'd been the only one that hadn't retaliated.

"I don't understand what's happening," Raven whispered, looking between Bianca and Kellen.

"The short version? There's bad Fae and good Fae. The bad guys are waging war on the good. We're trying to stop them before they take over Ireland. Just think...you could be the one who helps save the world," Bianca said, beaming at Raven.

"Um, that's a tall order methinks," Raven said, turning from Bianca as her gut churned with anxiety over her inability to make a decision. If she'd just been able to get some rest, she'd better be able to assess her choices.

An image of a cool bedroom entered her mind, and Raven stared into one of the Alicorn's eyes. It huffed out a breath, and nodded its massive head a few times, as though encouraging her to join them. Was he the one projecting the image into her head or was that her own delirious desires? A cool bedroom with nobody around was everything she wanted in this moment.

And to be safe.

Friends.

The word surfaced, and again, Raven was focused on the Alicorn. Perhaps, taking this risk would be worth it if she got to ride one of these beautiful creatures.

"Do I get to ride the Alicorn?" Raven asked finally, and Bianca gave her a relieved smile.

"Absolutely. And let me tell you, you'll never regret it. It's quite possibly my favorite thing about the Air Fae at the moment," Bianca said.

"Come on then. You're putting all of us at risk with your dallying," Kellen ordered, and leaned down to extend a hand to Raven. She balked, annoyed at his tone, but also at herself. He was right. If the Dark Fae had found her in this alley once, they could easily send backup. Every second counted. She could kick herself for delaying the inevitable. Reaching up, she grasped Kellen's hand, and jerked as that same spark of recognition rushed through her. Like an electrical current, or an adrenaline rush, she couldn't quite be sure, but the feeling was palpable when she touched him.

"Your guitar."

"I can't leave it," Raven twisted to look at him from where he'd positioned her in front of him. Maybe she was being stubborn, but she wanted to keep at least one piece of her life with her.

"Unhook it. It can come with us." Kellen's eyes weren't on hers, instead he held vigilant, searching the alley for threats as Raven slid the guitar off her shoulders. Once off, Kellen took it and slung it over his own shoulders before promptly grabbing her and tugging her tightly against him.

Between his legs.

A surprised puff of air left Raven as she was immediately cocooned by his large presence, his muscular legs cradling hers, one arm caught tightly around her waist. She squirmed, unused to being so close to another person, and his breath came hot at her ear.

"Don't fidget."

Oh. *Oh*.

Raven blinked, and before she could adjust to the new sensations that flooded her body, her world tilted.

And then they were airborne.

7

RAVEN

HAD she said she was tired? All traces of exhaustion left her body as the Alicorn hurtled through the air, dipping and diving at the lightest of touches from Kellen, all while Raven struggled to process what felt like a gazillion sensations at once.

They were flying.

Flying.

Hundreds of feet in the air.

The ground disappeared below them at a dizzying speed, Galway's busy streets shrinking until the people merely looked like a train of ants scurrying to their nest. The breeze blew her hair back, tickling her cheeks with a shock of cold air, and then they were through the clouds, damp mist clinging to their skin. Every time the Alicorn dipped on the wind, Raven's stomach tumbled with it, and if she'd eaten anything of substance in the last few days, she likely would have lost it. Instead, a burning knot of unease mixed with excitement settled low in her gut, and she held her breath.

"Breathe," Kellen instructed at her ear, and she shivered as his warm breath teased the damp skin of her neck.

"I *am* bloody well breathing," Raven shot back, even though she *had* been holding her breath at that particular moment. The air was tight up here, yet she still managed to breathe just fine, which was a question for another time. Kellen shifted, his muscular arm like iron around her waist, his hand lightly stroking her side. Did he even realize what he was doing? Her thoughts skidded between fear of plummeting to her death and the way his hand traced the sensitive skin. Over and over, he stroked her, like she was a nervous animal, and heat bloomed low in her body as she shifted once more between his legs.

"Must you keep fidgeting?" Kellen asked with a sigh, and then Raven felt why he was so annoyed.

Oh.

His hard length pressed against her back, right where she was nestled between his legs, and instantly her entire body flushed with heat. It was as though someone had thrown a switch, and no longer was she worried about death or Dark Fae. No. Now her only worry was what Kellen would do to her once they arrived, well, wherever he was taking her. By any indication, the man was attracted to her. Would he expect her to...perform for him? In exchange for her safety? If so, Raven would demand Bianca return her to Galway. There was no way in hell that she'd do something like that. Though she'd fallen on hard times in the past, Raven drew the line at exchanging sex acts for money. Not that there was anything wrong with that, she had many a friend who affectionately referred to themselves as "happy hoes," but it was a vulnerability issue for Raven.

She'd never been with a man before.

And she certainly wasn't about to start with some Fae prince or whatever just because she was dead on her feet, and he'd saved her from an attack. She could express her gratitude in other ways. But not with her body.

Raven gritted her teeth and held still, forcing herself to not think about the emotions that lay beneath her fear. Curiosity danced at the edges of her mind, and she viciously shoved the idea away. No. Now was not the time, nor the place, to suddenly become interested in sex. Raven blamed her lack of sleep for allowing her emotions to flirt this closely to lust, and slammed that door shut in her mind.

A raven darted by, cawing its greeting, and she was surprised to see a bird this high in the sky. That being said, she knew little about birds other than the fact that she'd always had a bit of an affinity for ravens. They were curious birds, often bringing her little trinkets and, because of her name, she often talked to them on her lonelier days.

"There's home."

At Kellen's words, Raven looked up to see, incredibly, cliffs spiraling out of a mass of thick clouds, hovering far above the earth, with various outposts built into the craggy rock walls. Raven's eyes widened, and she feared that if she blinked, the image would disappear, and she'd wake up curled in a ball on the sodden ground of the alleyway. There was, quite simply, no way this could be real. What was essentially a mountain floated in the sky far above Ireland, and Alicorns flitted around the outskirts like honeybees buzzing around a hive. It was unbelievable to the point of laughable, and a gurgle of laughter caught in her throat as Raven tried to wrap her head around what she was seeing. A strange keening sound arose, and Raven started when Kellen's arm tightened even more around her waist.

"You're not going to be sick, are you?" Kellen asked and Raven jolted, suddenly realizing the sound was coming from her.

"No," Raven said, faintly. "It's just so...this is your home? Like you live here? This is real, right?" Raven twisted to look at Kellen over her shoulder and froze.

Bad move, Raven.

Her lips were suddenly inches from his, and he regarded her with those steely eyes, and Raven wanted to squirm against the desire that tugged low inside of her.

"This is real," Kellen said. But his eyes were on hers, and Raven was caught, transfixed by the warm timbre of his voice, and the ease in which he cradled her against his body. Nobody had ever picked her up before, let alone held her close like she was a delicate package, and the feeling of being at his mercy left her both aroused and uneasy. She didn't like the shift in the power balance, and she didn't like feeling out of sorts. One of the reasons Raven had stayed so long in Galway was that she was rarely caught on her back foot, instead knowing all the inner workings of the city like the back of her hand. Now, a distinct unease filled her as the Alicorn landed gracefully in front of the tall pillars of a castle and Kellen jumped easily to the ground, with her in his arms. As soon as he let her down, she rounded on him, ready to mouth off to hide some of her nerves when a voice sounded behind her.

"This is what you left your city unprotected for? A girl? You had the king at your disposal and instead you fly off to pick up some chit? A human one at that? It's a disgrace you are, Kellen. Leaving your people like this. Again."

Kellen's jaw tightened, and if it was possible, his eyes turned even more icy. Raven whirled to see a man, much shorter than Kellen, but with enough resemblance for her to determine that he was, at the very least, a relative of Kellen's. Before Kellen could speak, Raven did what she always did when she felt uncomfortable—she went on the attack.

"Hardly a chit, old man. What are you? His servant? I'm surprised you let the help talk to you that way," Raven said to Kellen and was rewarded when the man's face flushed a deep red. A ghost of a smile slipped across Kellen's lips, and the sight only emboldened Raven.

"Yes, well, he's certainly impertinent," Kellen agreed.

"Impertinent!" the man burst out, spittle flying from his lips. "Have you lost your mind? You certainly aren't fit to rule if you let this...this..."

"Queen," Raven said, bowing her head in what she hoped was a stately manner. "That's Queen Raven to you. Queen of the Fringe People. From Galway."

The man just gaped at her, clearly uncertain how to

proceed, and Raven took that opportunity to push it further.

"You may see that a room is made up for me, as I'll be requiring rest and a bath." When the man did nothing, Raven gave him a steely gaze. "That was an order. Go on now."

"You can't possibly think that I'd..." The man stopped when Kellen stepped forward.

"Father. We rescued Raven at the king's request. Please be respectful to her while she is our guest."

"Guest?"

"Father?" Raven said at the same time, and the two stared at each other with equal amounts of annoyance.

"Queen Raven, please meet my father, Devlin of the Air Fae." Though Kellin's lips quirked at the use of her fake title, he didn't try to wash his father of the notion that Raven was anything but what she claimed. Points for Kellen on that one. He'd be useful in a grift if ever needed. Not that she was a grifter. She'd stolen before, but she didn't cheat people out of their money. It was a fine line, maybe only discernable in her head, but there was something about making a fool of people while you stole from them that was particularly distasteful to Raven.

"Charmed, I'm not," Raven muttered, glaring at Devlin.

"This is what you waste your time with? Your people need you." Devlin did spit on the ground this time, and Raven's lip curled in distaste. "And you bring a second human with you?"

Bianca and Seamus landed next to them, Bianca's face

brimming with joy, and she slid neatly off the Alicorn before smiling at everyone.

"I don't think that will ever get old. I mean, seriously. How cool is that? Riding on a flying freaking Alicorn? Seriously. *The* best." Bianca beamed.

"We're delighted to be your amusement ride," Devlin growled, and Raven's shoulders tensed.

"Your son just killed dozens of evil Fae. All while you were up here bloody well picking your arse for all we know. What, exactly, would you say it is you do around here? Because from where I'm standing it looks to me like if you were really all that worried about protecting your people from harm, then you'd be inside the castle walls doing just that, instead of keeping us out here, unprotected, and open to harm. Or perhaps that's your goal all along? Jealous you're not the ruler, is that it?" When Devlin's eyes flashed, Raven grinned. She'd found the mark. Now it was time to exploit it. "Ah, that's the truth of it, isn't it? You've got that little-man syndrome. Not as tall or as handsome as your son. And the people look to him for power, don't they? Not you? I'm not surprised if this is any indication of how you try to order people about. Now why don't you scamper along and go protect your people if you're so worried about it? Your help isn't needed here, little man."

When Devlin lunged, Raven was prepared for it, but to her surprise their Alicorn stepped between them and lowered its horn at Devlin.

"Riker," Devlin exclaimed. "You can't possibly be protecting her."

"Father. Please leave us. You've insulted all of our

guests. Some of whom, by the way, are honored friends of King Callum, having fought in the quest for the Four Treasures with resounding success. You owe them an apology."

Devlin's gaze held Raven's for a moment before he turned to Bianca and Seamus, his squat body all but vibrating with anger.

"My apologies," Devlin bit out. Raven wondered what the battle of the Four Treasures was. She'd have to ask Bianca about that later. Now, as the adrenaline from the flight wore off, Raven swayed on her feet and reached out a hand to steady herself on the Alicorn.

"Riker?" Raven whispered, ready to ignore Devlin and find the nearest bed. Maybe she could sleep next to this magnificent beast who had just acted as her protector. When the Alicorn turned and regarded her with warm eyes, Raven was pleased to see she'd gotten his name right. "Riker. That's a grand name. You're pretty damn majestic, by the way. Thanks for looking out for me. If nobody else does here, at least I know I can come find you."

The Alicorn let out a soft sound of happiness when Raven stroked its neck, and a cooling wash of energy moved through her, as though the Alicorn was gifting her with a mental reprieve from the altercation she'd just had. Leaning in, she pressed her forehead against his flank and looped one arm across his back, dead on her feet.

"Come on, Queen Raven. Let's get you to bed." Kellen's voice at her shoulder jolted her, and Raven realized she had quite literally started to doze off on a magical flying Alicorn.

"Sorry about that, Riker." Raven patted the Alicorn before accepting Kellen's arm. Not only did she need the support, but if he really was the ruler here well, then it wouldn't look so bad for her to enter the castle at his side. It was all about sending the right message to people, and Raven didn't want the message to the Air Fae to be that she was weak. Because she wasn't. But she *was* damn tired.

Kellen was silent as they walked through the gates of the castle, and Raven caught more than one Fae eyeing her with speculation in their eyes. She only raised her chin, meeting each gaze head-on, well versed in the game of street stare-downs.

"Thank you," Kellen finally said, and Raven jolted at his voice, turning to look up at him in surprise.

"For what? Picking a fight with your douchebag of a dad? I'm not sure that warrants a thanks."

"You stood up for me. You didn't have to do so. I'm used to my father's behavior. He's harmless, really. He's just–"

"A jerk?" Raven supplied as Kellen steered her into a roughly cut stone passageway. "Big ego...little..." She held up her pinky finger, and it took Kellen a moment to understand her meaning. His laugh rumbled from his chest, and the look of surprise on his face was like a reward to Raven.

"He's struggling to find where he fits in now that my mother is gone," Kellen said, reaching across Raven's shoulder to push open a wood door with floral etching.

"Well, shit. Now I feel like a right arse," Raven mumbled, her eyes widening at the beautiful room they'd entered. It was the same room that had been projected into her mind earlier, and she wondered if the Alicorn had done that or Kellen had. Either way, clean white marble lined the walls and the floor, and a large four-poster bed dominated the room. Ethereal robin's-egg blue gauze curtains were wound around the posts, draping and falling in such a manner that just looking at them soothed Raven. The room was coolly and calmly beautiful, and already the knots in her shoulders were starting to release. Turning, she looked up at Kellen.

"I'm sorry for your loss." Raven meant it too. She'd lost a lot on the streets, and it was just a way of life, but that didn't make it any easier.

"Thank you." Kellen's face was a mask, and Raven wasn't sure if she should press for more information or leave it. In the end, her time on the streets won out. People's secrets were their own, and if Kellen wanted to talk about his mother, he would.

"Is there...a place to wash up?" Raven asked instead, knowing she likely was not at her freshest after forty-eight hours on the streets.

"Yes, a washroom is through the curtain there." Kellen indicated a curtain, in the same blue as the bed. "Food and water is here. I'll make sure you're not bothered. After you rest, just come to the door and say my name. I'll hear it and lead you out of the tunnels. Don't try to explore them on your own. They burrow through the cliffs with an incredible number of twists and turns. Some end at the edge of the cliff with no way back. It's a security feature that can be deadly. If you prefer that Bianca comes to you, just call for me, and I'll bring her."

Kellen turned to go, but Raven grabbed his arm. Again, that tiny shiver of awareness ran through her when she touched him.

"Kellen. I suppose I owe you thanks."

"I don't know if you do. Yet. I'm still not entirely sure of your role in all of this. But I couldn't let you die, either."

With that, Kellen disappeared through the door, and Raven was left alone in the nicest room she'd ever been in. Unsure of what to do or if she should touch anything, Raven defaulted to self-preservation. Filling a cup with water, she downed it in two gulps before filling it once more. Food she was used to going without, so instead she took the cup with her and was delighted to find a modernly equipped bathroom. Stripping, she showered and then wrapped herself in a gossamer thin robe that somehow perfectly modulated her temperature.

The benefits of magick, and all that, Raven thought, carrying her cup to the bed. The sheets looked so pretty, with everything perfectly made up, that for a moment Raven considered curling up on an armchair tucked in the corner so as not to mess anything up. But in the end, her exhaustion won out, and she slipped beneath the lightweight blanket.

Sleep came instantly.

8

Raven

Raven awoke, moving seamlessly from sleeping to alert, as her past had taught her to do. For a moment, she blinked in confusion at the gauzy blue curtain draped above her head before it all came roaring back.

She wasn't in Galway anymore.

"Kellen," Raven whispered, bringing a hand to her lips, her first thought of the magnificent man whom she'd ridden with to this new place. Seconds later, the very man she spoke of materialized by her bed, a blur of movement so fast that Raven barely had time to register his presence.

Or the fact that the robe she'd gone to sleep in now gaped open.

Kellen's eyes moved lazily over her body, his gaze admiring, and Raven wanted to reach for him. Which was asinine, really, considering he wasn't even human. Grabbing the lapels of the robe, she pulled the fabric together and glared at him.

"Like what you see?" Raven glared at him.

"Yes. You're mouthwateringly beautiful. But you're also too thin, and it worries me. I'm hoping you'll eat today."

Raven's mouth dropped open as her brain struggled to formulate a response.

"It's not polite to stare at naked women." Which was the only thing it seemed she could come up with.

"You called me here while you were naked. What did you expect me to do?" Kellen arched a brow at her. "Besides, the Fae are far less fussy with nudity than humans are. We celebrate our natural form. It's not something to be hidden."

"Well, celebrate it from over there," Raven said, annoyed that she felt ridiculously pleased with his admiration.

"You've slept for a long time," Kellen said, crossing to where a plate of food sat next to the water pitcher. He poured a glass of water and lifted the plate before returning to sit on the edge of the bed. His nearness was disconcerting, and Raven was surprised to find herself wanting to lean into him where the mattress dipped under his weight. "I hope you're feeling refreshed."

"How long did I sleep for?" Raven asked, accepting the water from him. She resisted brushing a hand over her hair, knowing that she likely looked frightfully mussed.

"Eighteen hours."

"Eighteen—" Raven gaped at him. Surely, he was

lying. Never in her life had she slept for so long. "That's not possible."

"I can assure you, it is. But the color has returned to your face, and your eyes aren't so shadowed."

"Gee, thanks." Raven cast a glance at the washroom. Would she be able to slip out to use the facilities? No wonder she had to desperately relieve herself. But the last thing she was going to do was slip behind a curtain and use the toilet in front of Kellen.

"This offends you? My comments on your looks?" Kellen tilted his head as he studied her face.

"I'm not used to anyone offering commentary on anything other than my music." At the thought, Raven glanced around the room and was relieved to see her guitar case leaning against the wall.

"You'll have to play for me sometime."

"I don't *have* to do anything. Anyway, it seems like you have bigger things at hand. Speaking of which, is your dad ready to kick me out?" Raven asked.

"Don't worry about my father. I'll handle him." Kellen leaned forward and plucked a piece of cheese from the platter and handed it to her. Raven ate it without thinking, her eyes on the wall as she thought about Kellen's father.

"Is he always like that? In front of your people and all that? Can't be good for morale." Raven chewed thoughtfully. She'd known enough small-minded men with big egos like Devlin who liked to push others around.

"It's not. But again, something to be dealt with another time. Once you've eaten, I'll need you to get ready to come meet with us. We need to devise a plan of attack against the Dark Fae, and I can't have you as a loose end. I'll need eyes on you at all times."

"Excuse me? Am I a prisoner here then?" Raven turned to glare at Kellen.

"It's more for your safety. Can't have you toppling off the side of a cliff and falling to your death."

At the mere thought, a shudder ran through Raven as she was reminded that they hovered far over the earth on some weird cloud castle.

"Fine, but I need some time to get ready." Really, the need to use the toilet was becoming quite urgent. "Can you fetch Bianca for me? I could use some girl time."

Never in her life had Raven ever uttered the words "girl time" nor did she have the faintest idea what that actually entailed, but the request seemed to do the trick. Kellen stood and marched to the door.

"I'll have her sent at once. Your clothes have been cleaned and returned to you, along with other options in the same sizes."

With those words, Kellen departed, and Raven let out a long breath of relief. Once she was certain he was gone, she dashed from the bed and made quick use of the toilet, before splashing water on her face and taking a look in the ornate mirror that hung over the water basin. She was right, her hair was a fright, but Kellen had also been right—a healthy pink flush made her eyes look positively radiant this morning. The sleep had done her well.

"Hello?" Bianca called, and Raven ducked her head out of the curtain.

"Hi. I'm just getting dressed, and I'll be out. There's

food." With that, Raven pulled her head back in and studied the pile of clothes she'd grabbed. True to his word, her skirt and top had been cleaned, and her jacket even looked like it had been wiped of dust. The other pile of clothes that had been brought to her looked sharply expensive, the kind of clothes that rich people had custom-made for them, and she ran a curious finger across a pair of soft leather trousers. She supposed if they were going into battle and having to fly on Alicorns again, then the pants would make more sense.

Raven let out a soft sigh of delight as she pulled the pants on as they fitted like a glove. She crouched, feeling them give and move with her motions, and decided that they were the smart choice. Tulle skirts were great for performing, but likely not the best for battle. A dark purple tunic was next, which actually made her lavender hair look extra purple, and Raven almost whimpered at the soft wool against her skin. She honestly felt like a new woman, which didn't entirely sit well with her. Grabbing her jacket, she went into the main room and spied her boots. At least those could work well with her outfit.

"You look much better," Bianca said from the side-board where she picked at a pile of grapes. "That's a good color on you. You've kind of got this Lara Croft vibe going on now with the lavender hair and the leather pants."

"I have no idea what you're talking about…" Raven said, dropping into a chair and lacing up her boots. She was glad that she had tucked the contents of her pockets into the guitar case, for the Fae would have likely found her coins if they had cleaned her clothes without asking. A reminder that she had no real privacy here, Raven told herself, and was instantly brought back to her foster home days.

"Tomb Raider?" Bianca looked at her in question.

"Is that a show?" Raven raised an eyebrow at her. "I don't have a television. I never had one growing up either. I rarely watched television, have seen very few movies, and reading and music is my only form of entertainment."

"No television, huh? Why's that?" Bianca asked, a curious look on her face. Her energy wasn't judgmental, which Raven appreciated, so she gave the condensed version of her life.

"No parents. Raised in foster homes and then on the streets. Didn't have the budget for a place to lay my head. Let alone a luxury like a television."

"I'm sorry to hear that," Bianca said, her face serious. "When things die down, I'm going to introduce you to Tomb Raider. It's based on a video game, and there's this badass female lead called Lara Croft. She kicks serious ass. Tough as nails. You reminded me of her. Maybe it's the way you carry yourself."

The breath left Raven's body for a moment as she struggled with the unfamiliar emotion of wanting another woman to like her. As in, really like and admire her. What a friend would be like. She wasn't sure how to proceed, not with compliments like this, and she looked helplessly at Bianca.

Bianca, seeming to sense her awkwardness, prattled on.

"Anyhoo, there's loads of badass female characters. Well, actually, not as many as there should be. Sarah

Connor in the Terminator series is another one. We'll have a movie day one day and go through some of the good ones. I bet you're probably wondering what's all going on here, huh? It's wild, isn't it? This Fae world?" Bianca grabbed the plate of food that Kellen had left on the bed and offered it to Raven, who sighed before taking it. It seemed that everyone here was hell-bent on making her eat, so it would be rude of her not to. She'd long ago gotten over any awkwardness about accepting free food.

"I don't even know where to begin. I'm still tripping over the fact that we're floating on a castle in the middle of the air. If I think about it too long, I'll panic. I'm guessing it's what people feel like when they fly on a plane." Another luxury that Raven had never been afforded.

"Yeah, that's a riot, isn't it?" Bianca grinned and tossed her head, standing up to pace the room. "I used to give tours in Dublin when I was in university, all about the historical myths of Ireland. Little did I know that one day I'd find out that so much of the myths were based on reality. What do you know about the Fae?"

"Um, basically what I could get my hands on in the library." One of the few buildings that Raven could enter without being expected to spend money. The library, a bastion of knowledge and inclusiveness, and one of the only places she'd ever felt welcomed. It was where she'd learned about everything from songwriting to basic arithmetic. The librarians had always been kind to her and had looked the other way when she'd spent extra time in the bathroom freshening up. Raven liked to think they respected the fact that she actually read the books she asked for, plopping down at a table and devouring the pages from cover to cover. The fact that she'd been given enough basic schooling to learn how to read was the single greatest gift Raven had ever received in her life.

"Hmm, so brooding heroes and murderous rampages?" Bianca grinned when Raven looked askance at her.

"More like tricksters and you don't want to be upsetting them."

"Gotcha. You must not have gotten into the Fairy smut then." Bianca chuckled at Raven's expression. "Hey, don't knock it until you read it. I, for one, can attest to the magickal powers of having a Fae lover."

"Is this some sort of weird sex den that I've been kidnapped for?" Raven narrowed her eyes at Bianca, and the woman laughed, clearly delighted with Raven's humor. Though Raven hadn't been kidding. Why were they talking about sex when there could be an imminent war?

"Not in the slightest. Though the Fae are quite...free... with their love. Either way. Since you don't seem all that shocked about Fae actually existing, it seems I can skip forward to give you a quick overview of what we're dealing with?"

"Please." Raven fervently hoped there wouldn't be any more sex talk. Though she wasn't a prude, by any means, if there was danger coming her way she'd like to be as prepared for it as she possibly could.

"Right, so, let's see..." Bianca tapped a finger against her mouth as she thought about how to summarize decades worth of Fae history. "There are two sisters.

Goddesses. Danu is the goddess of all that is light and good, and Domnu is the goddess of all that is dark and evil. Centuries ago they had a terrible falling out and Domnu put a curse out, hoping to one day gain the greatest of powerful items—the Four Treasures. If Domnu could acquire those, she'd be all powerful and rule the world. Not just the Fae world. All of the world. We, and I mean myself, my honey, and those destined to seek and protect said treasures, defeated Domnu in her task about twenty years ago. She's a touch angry about that, if I must admit."

"She waited centuries to win, and you guys beat her? Yeah, okay, I'm guessing she's worked up a head of mad over it," Raven agreed. She ate a piece of fruit that was delectably sweet, and she glanced down to see what it was. It didn't resemble anything she knew about, and she wondered if it was a type of magickal fruit. The thought made her nervous and though she wanted another piece, she left the rest untouched on her plate.

"That she has. Now, she's trying a different tactic. See, Domnu has her own dark army—the Domnua. Those are the silver guys that keep trying to kill you. Danu rules the Danula Fae, which is what King Callum is. Between the two Fae lie the four elemental Fae factions. Each has their own ruling house, world, and they all work together to keep, well, everything in nature in balance. Domnu has taken it upon herself to disrupt the Elementals, seeking to gain allegiances, infiltrate, and upset each faction. Her goal is to sow distrust, get them fighting with each other, and to eventually rise up and take down the Danula Fae. It's another step toward getting what she wants, which is total domination."

"And we're meant to stop her?" Raven paused, a piece of cheese in her hand.

"That's the short of it, yes."

"Gotta find her weak spot," Raven muttered, chewing thoughtfully on the cheese, enjoying the way the taste mingled with the flavor of the fruit she'd just eaten. She didn't much know about fancy palates, but they paired really well together.

"Why do you say that?" Bianca asked, coming over with the water pitcher to refill Raven's glass.

"Um." Raven shrugged. "If you watch people carefully, you can figure out what they're playing at. Everybody, you know, they put on an act. They're posturing, I guess. Everyone has a weakness. It's an ego thing. The loudest guys are usually the most insecure, that kind of thing. Just gotta find her weak spot."

"You're not wrong," Bianca agreed. "But there's that whole immortality thing that makes it a bit trickier."

"Oh, right. What do you plan to do about that?" Raven looked up when Bianca laughed again. She liked this woman, Raven realized, and it made her feel just a touch uncomfortable. Bianca's easygoing nature seemed to suggest that Raven could trust her, but it wasn't in Raven's nature to take people at face value. For now, she'd sit back, observe, and ask questions. She also needed a moment alone so she could get her weapons tucked away in her pants.

"That seems to be the million-dollar question. My hope is that we've stumbled on a magickal ritual that could rid the world of her. I'm still researching though. Maybe, if we can't destroy her, we can effectively banish her or dissolve her powers. It's a tall order though."

"Does the sister help at all? You know, the good witch?" Raven gestured with her cup of water.

"Goddess Danu? She helps where she can. I think there's some pretty ancient rules that prohibit her from taking this on. I don't know though. Maybe we could request an audience and get some more answers. I'll ask King Callum about that." Bianca tapped a finger at her lips. "She might be our greatest resource if she's allowed to help us."

"Yeah, that. Why are you made to do the dirty work for her? It's her sister that's being a bitch," Raven pointed out.

"A major one at that." A knock sounded at the door. "Right. I think it's time to meet the others. Are you ready to go or do you need more time?"

"Go where?"

"Well, I think you'll probably want to look around a bit, no? And Kellen wants to have a talk with his people so we can devise a plan to protect the Air Fae. I think he wants everyone to be there, so we know what to expect. It's a touch trickier up here, what with not being on land and all that, and I know he's worried about you and me in particular."

"Because we'll fall off the edge and plummet to our deaths?" Raven scowled.

"Yes. The Air Fae have enough magick to fly short distances without their Alicorns. If they tumble off an edge they just pop back up. You and I do not have such luxuries, and as such, we're liabilities."

"Oh. Right. We're the weak ones." The thought didn't sit well with Raven.

"Never." Bianca gave a fierce smile. "We just let the men think that."

9

KELLEN

KELLEN SPENT over an hour in the stables, grooming the Alicorns, refusing to speak with anyone who approached him. His thoughts tangled around each other, and he needed silence to try and unravel the threads. He dearly wished he could take to the skies to clear his head, but then he'd be violating his own "No Fly" order that he'd issued. Though his people had grumbled about it, Kellen had promised them an update at some point today. Now he just needed to figure out what, precisely, that update would be.

The way he saw it—he had two choices.

Batten down the hatches and protect his people from an attack or take the offensive and ride into battle.

Neither felt particularly great, but he supposed that was the nature of difficult times. He'd come into leadership just as Domnu was stirring up trouble with the

Elementals, and now he'd have to deal with what came of the decisions he made.

Heavy is the crown, and all that.

It didn't help that he couldn't stop thinking about Raven. She was as skittish as a stray cat, inching away from him anytime he got too close, her moody eyes full of distrust. He wondered who'd hurt her.

And how he could fix it.

Kellen sighed and pinched his nose, frustrated with the direction of his thoughts. The last thing he needed to do was try and be a knight in shining armor for some human female. For all he knew, she could be a distraction sent to him by the Domnua. His thoughts skidded to Alistair, and his stomach twisted in knots.

At dawn, he'd held a small ceremony with Alistair's family. Nobody else had attended, though Kellen wasn't certain that anyone had been invited either. Alistair's family had taken the brunt of Devlin's accusations, with people shunning them and hurling insults as they just tried to grieve their only son. Kellen couldn't quite bring himself to accept that Alistair had been a traitor, and though the facts were there, he still didn't want his family to suffer. So he'd attended the ceremony, scattering flower petals in the wind as the soft rays of light bounced across the tops of the clouds, tinging them a soft pink. The petals had fluttered down, caught on the wind, as Alistair's mother had wept in Kellen's arms.

He feared there would be more dawn funerals if he chose poorly for his people.

"So this is where you're hiding out? Can't say I blame you. The Alicorns are badass."

Kellen jolted at the interruption, ready to unleash on whomever dared to interrupt him, when he realized it was Raven who'd come to stand outside the stall. Turning, he took in her appearance. Though he'd much preferred the naked and disheveled Raven he'd seen this morning when she'd called to him, he also appreciated this version of her. The leather pants hugged her legs, and the deep purple of the tunic brought out flecks of green in her stormy grey eyes. Her hair had been braided back on two sides, and she looked ready to take on the world.

"I wouldn't say that I'm hiding out," Kellen said, rolling his eyes at her. "I'm attending to their needs." Riker shifted at his side, letting out a soft sound that almost sounded like a laugh.

"Right, like none of the other gazillion stable boys you have running around here can't do that? You're *hiding*." Raven glanced around the stables, curiosity in her eyes. "Can't say I blame you either. Everywhere I go, people are talking about you."

"Where did you go? You were supposed to call for me to guide you." Kellen resisted asking what people were saying about him. He did not need or want to know. There was no reason to let their opinions weigh on his decision-making process.

"Bianca showed me around. Don't worry. Seamus was with us. As you can see, I didn't fall off the edge of the world or anything." Raven shrugged, her eyes still scanning. She was always watching, Kellen realized, always on alert. What kind of life had she led that had made her that way? "Cool place. Loads of tunnels and stuff, which would probably take ages to learn. But I like the architecture. And the people seem somewhat friendly even if they aren't sure what to do with me."

"Were people rude to you?" Kellen asked, surprised. He moved to lean on the stall door, and Raven automatically shifted away from him. If he didn't work as closely as he did with the Alicorns, Kellen probably wouldn't have even caught the movement, but he did, and instead wanted to soothe her.

"Mmm, not particularly. A few looked me up and down and closed their doors, that kind of thing. Your dad, man, he is just an absolute delight. Not sure how you put up with him." Raven shrugged nonchalantly.

"What did he do?"

"Nothing much. Just sneered at me and called me fake, I'm guessing because I'm not Fae. Don't worry, I put him in his place."

"What did you say?" Kellen sighed, though amusement danced at the edges of his annoyance.

"I just held up my pinky. And looked at his pants. He stormed off. It was quite fun, actually. I love making men like him upset."

"Have a lot of experience with that?" Kellen eased the stall door open and instead of stepping outside of it, he gestured for Raven to join him. For a moment, she hesitated, and he could see her actively weighing the consequences of being cornered in a stall with him, but the beauty of the Alicorn must have outweighed her concerns. That or she no longer considered him a threat.

Which pleased him, though Kellen wasn't quite ready to examine the reasons why.

"With what? Making small men with big egos embarrassed? Only a lifetime of it, doll." Raven threw her head back and laughed, though there was an edge to it, which intrigued Kellen. He wanted to unravel her stories, to find the core of Raven, and understand why he was so transfixed by her.

"Why?" Kellen asked, stepping back to give Raven space as she entered the stall. Riker turned to greet her, and a soft smile hovered on her lips as she reached out to brush a tentative palm against the Alicorn's side. Kellen instantly felt jealous of the animal. A breeze blew through the open door that led to the pasture on the other side of the stall, where Riker could come and go as he pleased, and Kellen caught sight of the other Alicorns milling about in the field. Riker must have communicated to them about taking safety measures, as normally at this time of the morning they would be taking to the skies for their exercise.

"Because when you've got nobody to vouch for you, men like your father see me as an easy target."

"What does this mean? Not having someone to vouch for you?" Kellen asked. Instead of drawing closer as he wanted to do, he leaned against the wall and crossed his arms while Raven grew more confident with petting Riker.

"Why are people always so interested in things that are none of their business?" Raven countered.

"Isn't that how we form bonds? I believe it's called getting to know each other. Becoming friends, even?" Kellen arched an eyebrow at Raven when she shot him an acerbic look.

"I wouldn't know," Raven muttered.

Kellen stayed silent, waiting her out, and finally she rewarded him with an annoyed sigh.

"*We're* not friends, Kellen. *I* don't have friends. Friends are...a liability. I've got acquaintances, okay? Like a team of people that kind of work together to help each other out but not, like, tell our deepest secrets to and have sleepovers and shit. It's not like that. *I'm* not like that."

"Who hurt you?" Kellen asked, finding that he desperately wanted to know. The wounded look that sprung into her eyes when she whirled on him made every bit of his inner protector scream to attention, and he wanted nothing more than to help her. Which was crazy, really, since he had his own problems to deal with. What Kellen needed to do was protect his people, not dally with some human who had zero interest in forming alliances with him.

"Who. Hurt. Me?" Raven enunciated the words with such careful precision and deadly cold anger that Riker shifted, stomping a hoof and nickering softly in warning. Kellen stepped forward to run a hand across the Alicorn's back to soothe him, though there wasn't much he could do for Raven. "Who *hasn't* hurt me, Kellen? Everybody lets me down. They always have. It's much easier to not trust anyone. So, really, at this point? Nobody hurts me anymore. They can't because I don't let them."

"Your family?" Kellen guessed, continuing to stroke Riker, hoping to keep Raven talking.

"My family? *What* family? I've been on the streets since I ran away from my last foster home. The closest thing I have to a family is my fringe family, Kellen. That's the people who live on the streets. We look out for each other. But we don't ask questions. And we never get too close. Do you want to know why?"

"Yes," Kellen answered honestly.

"Because when you're called to identify the body, your heart breaks. Over and over. After a while, you don't let yourself care anymore. It's much easier that way." Rage filled Raven's eyes, but no matter how much she postured that she didn't care, Kellen could see it. Deep down. She cared way too much. At her core, Raven was a vulnerable, broken woman, who'd never known love. It was something that, at the very least, he could be grateful to his own mother for. She'd never let him down, and he had to imagine the absence of a presence like that was catastrophic for a young child. Kellen took a moment before responding.

"That makes sense." Kellen kept his tone even. It wasn't sympathy Raven was asking for, and even though he felt it, Kellen wasn't going to offer it. "Do you know why Alicorns are so cool?"

"What?" Raven scrunched up her face in confusion. Clearly, she was expecting him to push his line of questioning.

"The Alicorns. Do you know one of the many reasons they are so cool?"

"Because they're flying magical badass unicorn beasts?" Raven asked.

"That, of course, is one of the many things that make them cool. Another is that there is no...how do I say it? Patronage? No, that's maybe not the word. Basically, Alicorns are born after the entire community looks after their nest.

They're quite literally grown and tended to by everyone. No mother. No father. It's a collective creation of new additions to their tribe. They all just look after each other."

"Really?" Delight filled Raven's face as she turned to wrap her arm around Riker's neck. "Is that really true? How can there be no mother or father?"

"It's magick. Ancient rituals. They decide together to bring in young ones. It's a mutual agreement, and they all take part in looking out for each other. Almost like planting seeds, I guess. Growing a garden."

"Fringe family," Raven muttered against Riker's neck.

"Want to know something else cool about Alicorns?"

"Naturally."

"They can communicate with you by putting images in your head."

"Really?" The last notes of the word went up higher, and Raven turned to him, giving him her first unrestrained grin. It almost toppled him over, the smile pushing away the lines of anger, and he realized he wanted to see more of her like this, with her walls down.

"Correct. Ask him something. With your mind, if you want."

"Okay, um, okay..." Raven danced back and forth, as excited as a kid about to open a present, and he wondered if she'd ever gotten gifts before. "Got it."

"Go ahead."

Raven closed her eyes and scrunched up her face like she was thinking really hard, and Kellen's heart seemed to sigh. What was he going to do with this impossibly contradictory woman? In some respects, she was as tough as his most hardened warrior and in others she was almost childlike in her innocence. The contrast was entrancing.

"Oh. Oh. Really?" Raven spoke to Riker, though she cast glances at Kellen, and he realized she must have asked the Alicorn a question about him.

"Pleased?"

"He says your dad is a butthole."

Kellen threw his head back and laughed, surprised that he could do so when so much weighed on his shoulders.

"I highly doubt that's what he said."

"Maybe I'm paraphrasing." Raven shrugged, her lips quirking. She stroked Riker's mane, and a worried look crossed her face.

"Will they get hurt? If there's danger?"

"They have magickal shields we've crafted to protect them. As well as their own magick. But I can't promise they won't. Which is another thing that weighs heavily on me." Kellen shifted, uncomfortable with speaking about his concerns to this slip of a woman.

"So, what's the plan then?" Raven asked. "You're going to go after the bad guys? Right?"

"Is that what you suggest that I do? People are relying on me for protection. As are the Alicorns. Do you think launching an attack is the correct choice?" Kellen had no idea why he was annoyed with her, yet he was. Or maybe he was just annoyed, in general, that he had to make this choice.

"Well, yeah." Raven shrugged and turned back to

stroke Riker. "In my experience, bullies don't stop, Kellen."

Bullies don't stop. He'd hardly call Domnu a simple bully. *But she was, wasn't she.* A bully was someone who hated to lose and fed off the weaknesses of others. Raven was absolutely right. The time had come for the Fae to be proactive. Thus far, they'd all been reacting to Domnu's moves and she continued to be one step ahead of them. It was time for them to see what they could do to put her on the defense.

"Then we have some plans to make. Let's go."

"Wait, me? Why am I involved?" Raven squeaked as Kellen stopped short of grabbing her hand and dragging her along before he remembered she didn't like being touched.

"Because the Domnua want you for some reason. You're probably an asset to us and we don't even realize it. We need to figure out how to use you to our advantage."

"That's cold, Kellen." Raven's eyes brightened. "But I like it. Exactly what I would do as well. Okay, let's use me as bait."

"Or let's not." Kellen was *not* going to use Raven as bait. But either way, he'd made his decision. He only hoped it wouldn't be one that he would come to regret.

10

RAVEN

"OH LOOK," Raven exclaimed when they left the stables. Instead of following Kellen toward the city, she detoured toward the pasture where two baby Alicorns raced at each other in a mock battle. "Babies! Oh my god, would you just look at that? I don't know when I've ever seen anything so cute before."

The two Alicorns locked horns, rising off the ground as their little wings fluttered, and the group of adult Alicorns surrounding them seemed to indulge their play. Raven jumped when a hand hooked her elbow.

"Careful. Not too close." Kellen pulled her back so they could watch from afar. "Though the Alicorns are our friends, they are very protective of the young ones. It's best to give them space."

"Oh. That's sweet," Raven said, her eyes caught on the tiny beasts who were now rolling in the grass. "They're seriously cute. I mean, when they're adults they are stunning and gorgeous and stately, but the little ones? They're kind of chubby and roly-poly aren't they?"

"They are. The baby fat burns off fairly quickly," Kellen said, a note of amusement in his voice.

A flash of silver caught Raven's eyes and she turned, a ripple of unease setting the fine hairs at the back of her neck standing. Reaching for the knife she'd tucked in her waistband, she turned from the pasture and stalked toward where she'd seen the light.

"What are you doing? We need to find Callum and get our plan together," Kellen insisted, keeping pace with her. "I don't have time to be chasing you all over. The tour portion of your day is through."

"Domnua," Raven hissed, and Kellen snapped into alert mode. Immediately, he positioned himself in front of her, and she almost tripped over his long legs and smacked her forehead into his muscular back.

"What the hell? Get out of my way."

"That's a hard no, darling. You're not facing off Domnua in front of me. I'll be the one protecting you," Kellen's voice had a cool undercurrent that somehow managed to both infuriate and arouse Raven. She dug an elbow into his back and poked her head around his arm, annoyed that he was blocking her view.

A sound came from behind her and the unease grew. Turning, Raven sucked in her breath. A wall of Domnua now separated them from the stables.

"Kellen."

"I'll not be arguing about this, Raven. Pipe down and let me handle it."

"Kellen," Raven said again, urgency in her voice.

"Hush, woman."

Raven rolled her eyes and bounced the knife back and forth between her hands, waiting for the Domnua to make their move. Behind them, the pasture had emptied, and Raven could only assume that the Alicorns had spirited the babies away to safety. At least she hoped so. Otherwise, she'd have to murder these Dark Fae several times over if they'd hurt one of the chubby baby Alicorns.

When Kellen let out a shout and leapt toward the Domnua, Raven did the same, knowing that he truly had no clue what they were up against. Typical man, thinking he had it all handled. Well, she'd just have to show him what she was made of, wouldn't she? Now that she was well-rested, Raven felt much more up for a fight.

"Well then, boys, let's see what you've got." Raven beckoned with one hand, lifting her chin with a smile. When the first jumped at her, she easily swept his feet out from under him and followed the movement with a knife to the back. Instantly, he dissolved in a puddle of silvery blood.

"Is that the way of it then? One stab and you guys explode? That's a precarious livelihood, isn't it? Or does it just matter *where* I stab you?" Raven beckoned the next forward and repeated the exact same maneuver. She came up, shaking her head in disbelief as a third followed the same pattern.

"You guys *are* dumb. I wonder how the Dark Goddess feels having such a stupid army. Is this just like, a battle of numbers then? Or does she send the eejits out first to test the waters or to see the weak points?" Raven slashed her way through a few more, humming cheerfully as she pivoted and kicked one in the back. Honestly, this was almost like a good workout. It was only when an arm came around her throat that her fun stopped.

"Damn it," Raven swore. Dropping her weight, she pulled the Domnua over her shoulder and flipped him to the ground, following with a stab between the eyes. Well, at least she felt like that is what she did. She couldn't quite bring herself to look at where she'd stabbed. She was tough, but even she wasn't a 'stab a person in the face and laugh' kind of tough.

At Kellen's shout, Raven turned and realized just how outnumbered he, well, *they* were. While he was certainly holding his own, the Domnua were being far more brutal with him than they were with her. Blood seeped from a cut on Kellen's forehead, and he stumbled back when a blade sliced his arm.

"Riker!" Raven wasn't sure why she'd called for the Alicorn, but it was the first thought that popped in her head as she ducked around the Domnua posturing in front of her, and raced toward Kellen. Surprising two of the creatures that had snuck up on him, she neatly drove her knife into each of their backs before whirling and pressing her own back to Kellen's. A large circle formed around them, but none of the Dark Fae moved again.

"Why did they stop?" Kellen asked, the muscles of his back heaving as he caught his breath.

"I don't know," Raven murmured. It had been like this the last few times she'd run into them as well. It was as though they wanted to tell her something. Raven could feel it in her bones. But now, a shriek split the air and Raven's eyes widened as Riker descended upon them, his wings fully outstretched, hooves in the air, his mouth open in an otherworldly scream. Fire shot from his horn like laser bolts, mowing down several of the Dark Fae, and Raven could have cheered in amazement. This was how she knew she was on the side of the good, Raven decided, when a miraculous beast such as Riker was willing to come to her defense.

When several of the army turned and brought arrows up, pointing them at Riker, Raven's heart skipped a beat. He wore no shield, even though Kellen had promised her he'd spoken with the Alicorns about protection. It was her fault. She'd called to Riker before he'd had time to protect himself.

So she did what she always did when she was in trouble.

Raven used her voice.

Pulling deep, she grabbed onto whatever that thing was inside her that made her powerful, and she screamed.

"Stop it! Stop this instant. Drop your weapons."

Instantly the Domnua did what she said, dropping their knives and bows.

"Raven. What's happening?" Kellen asked.

"Shh, just let me see if this will hold," Raven hissed. She held her hands out in front of her like she was conducting a sermon.

"Get out of here. This instant. Before we kill every last one of you," Raven ordered.

"I think we should do that. Kill every last one of them. Why let them get away?" Kellen argued at her ear.

"I have no idea. What if they stop listening to me as soon as we start trying to kill them again?" Raven whirled on him, exasperated. But it was hard to keep up her anger as blood streamed down his handsome face. "Damn it, Kellen. You're bleeding everywhere."

"Sorry?" Kellen said, a wry look on his face.

In seconds the field was empty of Domnua, aside from a few pools of silvery blood that seeped into the ground, and Riker trotted forward, huffing out a breath as he brought his head near Raven's.

Safe?

Raven realized that Riker was sending her a message, and she nodded to the Alicorn while reaching up to pat his neck.

"Yes, Riker. I think so. I'll get this one bandaged up. You go check on those chubby babies of yours. Stay on guard though, okay? I don't want to have to worry about you guys too."

"Why are you acting like you need to take care of me?" Kellen demanded. "I'm the one in charge here."

"Says the man dripping with blood. I don't see a drop on me. Or, if I do, it's likely yours." Raven glanced down to make sure that Kellen hadn't ruined her new outfit.

"What was that voice trick you did? You used it on me once before. It's time you tell me what your magick is, Raven. I can't go into battle with an unknown at my side."

"Seems to me that you just did. And this unknown just saved your sorry arse." Raven smiled when Riker nickered, seeming to laugh with her, and she took off in the direction of the castle. "Come on, pretty boy, let's get you sorted."

"Pretty boy? You think I'm pretty?" Kellen's voice was caught between pleasure and annoyance and Raven rolled her eyes, tossing him a look over her shoulder.

"Right now? You're a bloody mess. Let's find Bianca before you scare the children."

"You still didn't answer my question." Kellen caught up with her, and Raven had to stop herself from reaching out to check his wounds. That was something that a friend would do. And they weren't friends. They were... well, she didn't really know what they were. Or why she was here. It was best not to form any real alliances until she understood her role in this world.

Except for the Alicorns, that is. She'd be friends with them all day long.

"I gave you my answer, Kellen. I don't know what it is. I've never known. It just *is*."

With that, the royal guard met them, and Kellen was surrounded. It was easy enough for her to slip to the back of the crowd and lean against a stone wall. From there, she'd be able to watch the crowd for any suspicious activities.

Like when Devlin arrived and saw his son was hurt.

Instead of rushing to his side, he sneered and whispered to some of the onlookers, gesturing to where Kellen's blood was being mopped up. It didn't take a lip reader to see that he was pointing out why Kellen shouldn't lead.

"What happened?" Bianca asked, arriving at her side with a slender woman with big eyes and brown hair.

"Domnua attacked."

Bianca followed Raven's gaze.

"His father doesn't seem too fussed about it," Bianca pointed out and Raven smiled, knowing that despite her no-friends lifestyle, she might just very well like Bianca.

"My thoughts exactly."

11

Kellen

Kellen's blood was raging.

He wanted to act. To do *something*. Not just because his Alicorns had been put in danger again, by the Domnua, but because Raven had been as well. Or maybe it was just the adrenaline kick after a fight, but Kellen wanted to seek Raven out, to pull her close, to sink into her softness.

Not that she was all that particularly soft. She only showed him her hard edges, but he'd caught glimpses of her carefully hidden vulnerabilities. Either way, Kellen was even more intrigued by this woman he'd plucked off the streets of Galway. Who was she really? And what magick did she carry?

He believed her when she said she didn't know what her magick was. Of course, there actually wasn't much reason for him to believe her, but at the same time, she'd given him no reason not to. It was a strange place to be in, this push-pull between wanting someone and suspecting they might be sent to hurt his people. That being said, she'd killed for him. If she was part of the Domnua, she certainly wouldn't have killed her own people.

The reality was, Kellen was in reaction mode. And that just kind of made him angry. It was hard to feel like a leader when he was simply responding to events as they unfolded, instead of taking control of the direction they needed to go in.

"Kellen. How bad is it?" King Callum entered the room where Kellen had gone to escape the crowd. He needed a moment to clear his head before he did something impulsive.

Like throw Raven over his shoulder and take her to his bedroom.

"It's not so bad. Stings a bit, but they patched me up quickly enough." Kellen shrugged. That was the way of Fae healers. They were lucky enough to have magick on their side when it came to closing up wounds. Though it wasn't immediate, Kellen would barely have a trace of a scar by morning. That being said, he was just lucky that the Domnua hadn't used an insidious poison on their blades. Sometimes, when spells seeped into the bloodstream, they were difficult to counteract.

"I'm sorry to hear it. I'm told it happened near the stables. Do we know where the breach was?"

"Not yet. I've just finished with the healers. I'm hoping to speak with—"

"Sir?" One of the Royal Guard poked his head in the door. "I'm back from my scouting mission."

"Please, come in. What did you find?" Kellen gestured for the man to take a drink from the side table, but his guard only stood at attention and rapid-fire delivered his message.

"We discovered a breach in the wards on the southeast corner. It is, of course, being rectified as we speak. It was enough to allow the Domnua through."

"Can you tell how it was breached?" King Callum asked, and the guard swallowed.

"It's...it's hard to say, sir. But judging from the pattern of magick, it seems to have been broken from the inside."

"From the inside?" Callum's voice rose. Protection spells, like those in the wards surrounding the Air Fae's castle, were intricately woven, almost like a net or a spider web. It was easier to unravel such spells from the inside than it was from the outside, as their strength lay in keeping the undesirables out.

"It's hard to say, definitively, as we worked quickly to repair the hole. But, from my personal estimation, yes. I believe that someone with strong magick allowed the Domnua inside."

Raven.

For some reason, Kellen's thoughts jumped to the lavender-haired songstress, and he wondered if she'd slipped away in the night and broken his wards. She had magick, of that he was certain, yet she'd been dead on her feet when Kellen had brought her here. Had it been possible that it was all an act?

"Thank you. Please take extra care today in strengthening all wards. Alert the people we'll be having an announcement in one hour's time." With that, Kellen dismissed the guard and turned to Callum.

"You have a traitor in your midst," Callum said, pressing his lips together. Instantly, Kellen opened his mouth to make his apologies, but the king held his hand up to stop him. "I understand. We did as well at our castle. It's likely most of the Fae realms do, unfortunately. It's better to know than to operate on the assumption that we don't. It's...unfortunate. But that is the reality of what we're dealing with."

"I want to fight," Kellen said, turning to Callum with his fists clenched. "I don't want to sit and wait for her to make her next move. I say we go. To the Dark Realm."

"Attack on her turf?" Callum crossed his arms and considered Kellen's words.

"What are the other options? Wait for her to show up? Lure her out of hiding? Or go knock on her door."

"Bianca found a ritual—"

"That requires all four amulets. I don't have mine. It would be an incomplete ritual." Kellen turned and began to pace the room.

"It would. But that doesn't mean it wouldn't have some effect. It might not take her out, but it could weaken her. Maybe we could try for a multi-layered approach. Weaken her with a ritual. Attack in her realm. And... whatever other magicks that Lily and Bianca have unearthed with their research?"

"Can we get Danu here? Will she give us an audience?" Kellen asked.

"I'm not certain how much she's allowed to intervene. Otherwise, she would have stopped this long ago, no? But it's worth a shot," Callum admitted. A knock sounded at the door, and Lily poked her head inside.

"Permission to enter?" Lily's face warmed at the sight of Callum, and Kellen felt that small stab of loneliness again.

"You're always welcome, my love." Callum strode forward and all but dragged Lily into the room, followed closely by Bianca, Seamus, and Raven. Raven walked directly to him, hands on her hips, and looked him up and down.

"You look well enough then," Raven said.

"No scars to make me look more dashing," Kellen agreed.

"Shame. Would have taken some of the pretty off you." Raven sneered slightly.

"Ah, she still thinks I'm pretty." Kellen grinned, clutching at his heart, and Raven rolled her eyes before turning away. He wasn't sure why he cared what she thought about his looks, but he was taking her words as a compliment.

"We think there's a traitor here as well," Callum said without preamble, and Kellen caught a look between Bianca and Raven.

"What's that look for?" Kellen demanded, pointing to the two women.

"Nothing." Raven shrugged.

"I think we're both just watching," Bianca said. "Trying to get a read on things. We're outsiders, so maybe we see things differently. But your people are not united."

"No, they're not. They've had a hard time after my mother passed. As have I," Kellen admitted. "I fear I've let them down by not being as fierce a ruler as I should have been."

"You're doing the best you can," Callum said, surprising him with a hand on the shoulder. "We all are. Ladies, thoughts on doing your magickal ritual without all four amulets? We've decided to launch a counterattack."

"Badass," Raven commented, dropping onto a chair and crossing her legs. She tugged at one of her braids as she watched him with eyes that gave nothing away.

"I mean...I can't...say...really," Lily stammered, wringing her hands. "It might not be safe? I don't know enough about magick."

"Luckily, I'm well trained." Callum smiled down at her. "I'm of the opinion that the spell would be strongest with all amulets, but intent also matters. Perhaps we could find something of equal importance to the Air Fae and offer it as their contribution to the spell?"

"A substitution. Not unheard of," Bianca agreed, eyes brightening. "That's the nature of magick, right? Intent above all. Ingredients subject to change."

"Oftentimes, yes." Callum gave a curt nod.

"Not a bad idea. When are you thinking of doing this? We'll need some time," Bianca said.

"Plus you'll need to get the others on board. We're operating on the assumption that all of the Elementals will be open to giving up their amulets," Seamus pointed out.

"Right, there's that too. So, can we call them here? Talk it out?" Bianca raised an eyebrow at Callum.

"We're launching a two-pronged attack. Possibly even

three. One, we want to unleash the power of the ritual. The second will be us invading her realm. The third would be, well, if we could get Danu involved," Kellen said. Bianca turned to him.

"If we can get her blood, you mean? That's a tall order."

"Maybe she doesn't have to give it to us. Maybe she can be the one who executes the ritual," Lily suggested. "We can ask, can't we?"

"What's this blood stuff?" Raven asked.

"We found some ancient manuscripts that suggest there are ways to kill a god or a goddess. That immortality is not, in fact, automatically a given. But, it seems that only those who carry the blood of the god or goddess can enact the ritual."

"Or give the killing blow," Lily added.

"Wait, you mean Danu could just kill her? She doesn't have to do a blood ritual?" Seamus asked in surprise. "She could have saved us a lot of time."

"I don't think it is that simple. Translation is tough," Bianca admitted. "Ancient scripts aren't easy to read, and they wear with age. But, maybe?"

"What's the blood ritual entail?" Raven asked.

"It's all very dramatic. Blood of my blood, cutting of cords, like cutting the head from a beast," Bianca said. "I don't think we even *have* the entire ritual. But it's a big deal. Which, I guess, it has to be. She's a freaking almost-immortal goddess."

"So why not try and convince Danu to take her out?"

"Maybe because she's just as likely to get taken out?"

Raven offered and everyone turned to look at her in surprise.

"What do you mean?" Lily asked.

"Listen, rule number one in the streets—don't take on a fight that you can't win. If Danu can kill Domnu, it's likely the same on the flip side. And if Danu is the good one, well, she probably has a conscience about actually killing her only sister. Whereas Domnu would probably happily take her sister out with no problem. Danu making herself scarce? She's not doing it to be a jerk. She's doing it out of self-preservation. At least that's my take."

"That's...an excellent point," Bianca muttered. "Annoying, because it almost seemed like we'd have an easy out with Danu. But nothing in life comes easy, does it?"

"Right. So back to the four-amulet ritual and an attack in her realm. What specifically are we trying to accomplish in the Dark Realm?" Seamus asked. "Just so I know what my mission is?"

"Weaken her army. Make them not trust her. Make it so they are less likely to do her bidding. Some of what she's doing up here. But when we go, we go big. We take out as many as we can," Callum said, shaking his head with a look of regret on his face. "Not that I ever advocate for killing huge amounts of Fae, but—"

"They're not like you anyway," Raven interjected, and again the room turned to her in surprise. "What? You guys said you were fighters. Don't you analyze the opponents? They're not bright. At all. If anything, they're merely puppets. I haven't had as much interaction with them as you have, but they just seem to be following the motions. I don't think they have the capacity for quick thinking. If that makes it any easier to take them out."

"It might," Callum said, a smile quirking his lips. "It's kill or be killed at this point. The time has come for force."

"So? We're agreed? Call the other Elementals here? Figure out the ritual? Invade the Dark Realm? What's our timeline?" Kellen looked around the room.

"Two days' time. Enough to prepare, but not give away what we're doing to Domnua."

"Let's inform the people."

Raven made a loud buzzer sound, and Kellen gaped at her.

"What was that?"

"Wrong answer, boyo. You've got a traitor, and you're just going to go tell everyone your plans? I think you might want to review that decision." Raven circled a finger in the air by her head.

"She's not wrong. Can you ready your army without revealing too much?" Callum asked.

"Just misdirect them. Tell them you're going to...I don't know, someplace else. Or that you know she's coming and you're getting ready. You can make it look like you're preparing for something else but be ready to move. You have to stay one step ahead here," Raven said, and Kellen just looked at her, and wondered what kind of life she'd lived that made her able to assess a situation in such a manner. He needed to ask her what she meant about life on the streets, but that would be for another time.

"Tell them I'm calling the armies to the Danula Castle. That we're gathering there in three days' time," Callum suggested, and Raven nodded her approval.

"Now you're thinking smart."

"I'm so glad you approve." The king of all the Fae raised an eyebrow at Raven, and she beamed at him.

"Happy to help. I'll be here all night."

12

RAVEN

"YOU'RE COMING WITH ME."

Raven raised an eyebrow at Kellen's words. She'd rather go along with Bianca and help research the ritual. Surely, they could use all the help they could get with digging through the old manuscripts. But there was something in Kellen's tone that brooked no disagreement. Which was unusual for her, and Raven felt annoyed as she followed Kellen from the room.

"Yes, sir. Whatever you say, sir. At your service, sir." Raven put a jaunty note in her tone, needling Kellen as she followed him down a pathway that led deeper into the mountain. It annoyed her even further when he didn't respond to her baiting, so she stepped it up a notch.

"Is that what all the ladies do? Just follow you around at your command? Must give you quite the ego, right?"

Kellen stopped at a door and held his palm to a

carved slot. A click sounded and Raven realized that he'd unlocked the door with just his hand. When she followed him inside, an uneasy feeling rose. If the only way in was through a palm scanner, then...

The door slammed behind her, and Raven stilled, her senses on alert. She affected carelessness.

"Bet the women love that little party trick."

"What is with you?" Kellen whirled on her and stalked forward until Raven's back was against the wall. Her pulse hammered in her throat, and she forced herself to breathe evenly as he loomed over her, readying herself to fight if necessary. "Why the constant need to push and push? I've done nothing to you other than *help* you. Yes, I needed you to come with me. I'm the ruler here. I'm used to giving commands. It's not an ego thing. It's just the way of it. You tell people what to do as a leader. That is what they look for."

"You're not *my* leader." Raven lifted her chin, meeting his stormy gaze.

Kellen placed his hands on either side of Raven, not touching her, but caging her, nonetheless. Instantly, she stilled, watching for the slightest indication that he would move to hurt her.

"The only reason that I haven't told anyone about your little voice trick that you do is because I'm hoping you'll still tell me where your magick comes from. I'm going to ask you one last time, Raven. *Who* are you?" His voice, though firm, held a note of exhaustion, and it was that which caused Raven to relent.

"I don't know." Raven's voice caught. "I'm not lying when I tell you that. I truly don't know. I've tried, trust me, I've tried over the years. Tried to track down any trace of information about who I am. Where I came from. Nothing. I've got nothing. I just think that I might be—"

"Part Fae? Magickal? Do you come from our realm, Raven?"

"I just told you that I don't know, didn't I?" Raven ground out, frustrated with him pushing her to reveal her deepest vulnerabilities. It wasn't particularly fun to tell him that nobody cared about her. That not a single person had seen fit to claim her as their daughter or bothered to raise her.

"Your voice. It has power. Why? What can you do with it?" Kellen kept her there, pinned to the wall, his interrogation not complete.

"I...I don't know. Not really," Raven insisted when Kellen shook his head, dismissing her words. "I'm serious. I don't know. I just...listen. It started when I tried copying the confident people. The ones walking down the street that people moved out of their path. The ones who walked into restaurants and everyone watched. I copied how they spoke. The way they asked for things. How they expected people to do things for them. It was just a..." Raven fluttered her hand in the air. "An affectation at first. A way to try and gain some sense of confidence when I didn't have a leg to stand on. Then I just learned that I could be really, really good at using my voice if I tried. That's it. I don't know about magick or spells or rituals. I just know that sometimes, if I try hard enough, I can make people do what I want."

"An enchantress," Kellen muttered. Raven pushed his chest, needing to move, to pace, but he didn't budge.

"I'm no enchantress. I just told you that I don't know magick."

"And yet, you use it without thinking, carelessly even."

"How would you know how I use it? For all you know I'm using it to get people to feed hungry kids," Raven said, anger making her stomach turn. How dare he assume that she would use her voice for evil?

"There's a traitor in our midst, Raven. The Domnua we killed today? They broke the wards. The spell was ripped from the inside. Is that something you want to tell me about?"

"You can't be..." Raven threw her head back and laughed, disbelief joining anger in her gut. "You...you think that I, of all people, snuck out and ripped a hole in your magickal shields and then waited to get attacked by the Dark Fae? To what purpose?"

"I'm not sure," Kellen admitted.

"Listen, boyo." Raven jabbed a finger into Kellen's chest, anger winning out. "*You're* the one who dragged me here. I was doing just fine on my own. I didn't ask to come to your stupid world with your stupid problems. I have enough of my own."

"And yet, here you are."

"Well, you had freaking Alicorns, okay?" Raven kicked his shin in frustration and a ghost of a grin crossed Kellen's gorgeous face. He leaned forward, until his face was inches from hers, and Raven was torn between wanting to headbutt him and kiss him.

Which, in itself, was so shocking that she automatically made a move forward, but he grabbed a braid and jerked her head lightly back.

"Careful, darling. I'm not in the mood for another head injury at the moment."

"Then I advise you get your face out of mine." When Kellen didn't move, instead just staring at her while he held her braid, the air shifted around them, as though the particles that held anger and distrust were whisked away, and something else moved into the room.

Curiosity.

The possibilities of new beginnings.

It was almost intoxicating, *almost*, but Raven reminded herself that this man had just accused her of being a traitor, so that certainly wasn't the best way to gain her affection. Though she did give him points for being direct. In any other situation, she very well could have been tried and accused without anyone asking her if she was guilty or not. Because, at the very least, he'd asked her and had actually listened to her response, she decided not to knee him between the legs.

"I'm sorry you have a traitor. But it's not me. I was dead asleep for however many hours and then I was with Bianca or you the entire time. I haven't been alone. Even when I came to the stables, Bianca dropped me off. It's not me you're looking for, if that's your concern."

With those words, Kellen eased back, finally dropping his hands, and breaking the moment. Turning, he stalked away, and Raven let out a breath that was, admittedly, shakier than she had expected it to be. For more reasons than one. Now that Kellen wasn't blocking her view, she took in the contents of the room.

"Holy shite..." Raven breathed, turning in a circle. Weapons of all shapes and forms lined the walls, some of which were beyond anything she could have imagined. The arsenal went far past knives and bows, and all sorts of instruments, with varying degrees of menacing capabilities, were on display. At one end of the room, mother-of-pearl shelves held intricate bottles with liquids and powders of all colors. "This is quite a collection."

"Yes, well, the Fae have been around a long time. We've had time to collect our favorites." Kellen stood in front of one particularly gruesome-looking dagger, which resembled a mini trident, and sighed. Raven felt the anger drain from her body as Kellen's shoulders slumped.

"Hey, listen, it's going to be okay. You've got some good people on your side."

"I wish my mother was here."

You and me both. Raven walked closer, stopping short of touching him, and studied his face.

"Do you want to tell me about her?"

"She was everything. Joyful. Fun. Commanding. Terrifying. Both sides of the coin, I suppose you would say. People adored her. And trusted her to make the right decisions. Now I'm wondering if I'm making the right choices. Is going into battle the right move? My people could get seriously hurt. I've already lost Alistair." Kellen's voice cracked, and Raven did something she never, ever, did. Reaching out, she ran a hand lightly across Kellen's back, soothing him, as she looked up at his face.

"Your mother sounds like she was a pretty cool lady. As for the battle stuff, well, it's not just you. The king is making the choice as well. You're working as a team, with all the other factions of Fae or whatever the others are called. You don't have to take it all on yourself. You're *all* making this choice together. Which you kind of have to, right? It's not going to stop unless you do."

"Some of my people will die." Kellen's voice held a bone-deep sadness.

"Yes, unfortunately, that's unavoidable in battles. But, I guess the question is, will more people die if you let her win?"

Kellen turned and gave her a measured look.

"Yes, they would."

"Then I think you have your answer."

"I'm worried," Kellen admitted.

"A good ruler should be." Raven eased back. "That means you care."

"My mother cared as well."

"And your father?" Raven kept her tone light though she wanted to scream at him that he really needed to put his father in his place, or the man would derail everything they were working toward.

"It's hard to say. I can't decide if he is more interested in having power than he is in using the power for good." It was a brutal admission, coming from a son, and Raven watched the sadness settle onto his face. "They were never fated mates."

"Fated mates? Who? What is that?" Raven turned and reached out to touch the dagger, but he slapped her hand away. "Hey!"

"It's magicked. Every piece in here is. You can't just

pick the weapon up and use it, otherwise you'll come to great harm."

"Would have been useful to tell me that from the start, no?" Raven muttered, annoyed. Now she wanted to pick up every weapon in there, precisely because she'd been told that she wasn't allowed to touch.

"Fated mates are vitally important in the Fae realm. Not everyone finds theirs. Some are fine if they never do. Others claim their mate and the claim isn't returned. Those perish. But if two claims are met? It's an incredible bond, one that enhances both magickal powers and longevity. It's a deeply revered tradition among my people."

"Oh, wow, like super-charged soul mates?"

A trace of a smile crossed Kellen's lips as he turned to look down at her.

"Something like that."

"And dear old papa wasn't your mother's fated mate. Hmm, I wonder why she chose him then?" Raven pressed her lips together, immediately feeling bad when Kellen winced. "I'm sorry. Sometimes I speak without thinking. Just tell me to shut up."

"Shut up," Kellen said.

"See, that shouldn't be charming, and yet for some reason it is."

"So, I'm pretty *and* charming? Your opinion of me grows fonder."

"Don't flatter yourself." Raven turned away to hide her smile. Warmth bloomed inside of her, a decidedly unusual feeling for her, and she went to study the shelves of bottles, keeping her hands locked behind her back so she didn't reach out and grab one. It was hard to resist the urge, as each bottle was more magickal looking than the next, and she'd never been in the presence of such beauty before. Master artisans must have crafted these bottles, Raven mused, her eyes lighting on one that was formed to look like two dragons twining around each other. "No fated mate for you then?"

She didn't know why she asked. It wasn't any of her business, nor did she really care. But information was power, Raven told herself, as she continued to study the bottles.

"No." Kellen was at her back, his voice a warm timbre, and the fine hairs on the back of her neck stood up.

"Not looking for one or just haven't found her?" Raven asked, edging away from him a bit even though her body, surprisingly, was urging her to lean backward into his. *Stupid chemical reactions.* That's all this was. Close proximity to a hot guy in a dark room. Simple chemistry.

"I'm not certain I'm meant to have one." The answer relieved Raven, and then she was immediately annoyed at herself. Why would it relieve her? It's not like the freaking ruler of the Air Fae would suddenly fall in love with her and she'd become a magickal princess. Even with the knowledge that magick existed in this world, Raven had learned long ago that fairy tales didn't happen for girls like her.

"Probably for the best." Raven turned and pasted a smile on her face. "Relationships are nothing but a distraction. That's the last thing you need before you go into battle."

"Perhaps. Not a sentimental type, are you, Raven? Not

one to dream of love?" Kellen reached behind her and grabbed a bottle from the shelf, pocketing it in the jacket he wore.

"Not one to dream," Raven amended. "That's one luxury I certainly can't afford."

"That's a pity. Dreams can shape your future."

"*I* shape my future," Raven said, bringing a finger to her chest. "Not dreams. Not wishes. Do you know how many nights I wished for my life to be different? Guess what? Wishes do nothing. The only person who changes my life is me. You can take your dreams and shove it."

"Why—"

They were cut off by a knock at the door and Kellen turned, distracted.

"We must go. It's time to speak with my people."

13

RAVEN

"YOU SHOULD BE the one making the announcement."

Raven raised an eyebrow at Devlin, who had pushed her behind him and stood next to his son while King Callum addressed the crowd of Fae.

"Why? He's our king. Callum has every right to address our people."

"It makes you look bad. Weak."

"It certainly does not." Kellen turned away from where Callum spoke to the crowd and glared down at his father. "Why? *Why* are you always putting me down? You question every decision that I make, you're breathing over my shoulder everywhere that I go. Don't you trust me to take care of our people?"

Raven looked around, vaguely wishing she had a bucket of popcorn, and waited to see if Devlin would react predictably. In her experience, men like him rarely reacted well when confronted.

"This isn't about trust. It's about being a leader, Kellen. You need to show everyone that you're the one in charge." Devlin deflected the question.

"You don't, do you? You don't think that I can do this? That I can lead our people. Do you honestly think that mother didn't train me well enough for this position?"

Raven pursed her lips, studying Devlin's face when Kellen brought up his mother. For a moment, a hint of pain shadowed the man's eyes, and then his emotions were hidden once more.

"Of course I think you can do this job, Kellen. Why do you think I push you so hard? It's because of your mother, not despite her. I want you to honor her name. She was a great leader, and I want you to be too."

"But you don't think I am yet."

"Nobody is when they first start out." Devlin dismissed Kellen's statement. "But if you can't handle me questioning you, well, perhaps you're not ready to be a leader. Because every great ruler will be challenged at some point. I'm the least of your worries."

Something flashed in Devlin's eyes, causing Raven to tilt her head and study the man more closely. He reminded her vaguely of a guy she used to know on the streets. He was a grifter of the greatest level, wheeling and dealing with all the charm of a movie star. Most people never even knew they'd been taken advantage of. Devlin had that same look in his eyes. So, what was his game? Did he want to be ruler himself or did he just want to be the one pulling the puppet strings? Either way, Raven could feel Kellen's frustration radiating from him.

"I need you to be an ally, father. Not a hindrance."

"A hindrance?" Devlin scoffed and turned back to the crowd where Callum was finishing his instruction. Raven could no longer see his face. "Hardly. My greatest wish is to see you succeed."

Liar, liar.

"Then you'll have no problem coming to battle with us."

"What?" Devlin turned, shocked. "I'm an older man. I should be staying here to protect the women and children."

"Half the women are coming with us. They're equally as capable in battle as the men are," Kellen pointed out as he turned away from the crowd. He surprised Raven by hooking his arm through hers, and she resisted automatically pulling away from him while Devlin was watching. "Let's go find Bianca and Lily."

With that, Kellen all but dragged Raven away, but she couldn't help turning back to look at Devlin who watched them leave with an undecipherable look in his eyes.

"Do you think he means that? Is he just one of those stage manager type fathers?" Raven asked as Kellen pulled her easily through a winding maze of tunnels.

"I have no idea what you're saying to me."

Raven realized that they probably didn't have talent shows and the like in the Fae realm.

"Um, just like overly fussy about making sure you succeed?"

"Seems that way," Kellen muttered.

"That's tough, I'm sorry. Maybe he'll ease up once you win the battle and stuff," Raven said, following Kellen into a room with long tables covered in books. Lily and

Bianca sat across from each other with several manu-scripts unrolled in front of them.

"Maybe." Kellen's tone was biting, his shoulders stiff. She couldn't really blame him. She didn't like people telling her what to do either.

"Ladies, I'm bringing Raven to join you while I meet with Callum to discuss our plan of attack. You'll look out for her?"

"Meaning you'll babysit me?" Raven arched an eyebrow and plopped into the chair next to Bianca. "Don't worry, Dad. I'll be on my best behavior."

"I certainly hope so. I have enough to worry about."

With that, Kellen disappeared, taking his broodiness with him. The three women watched him go in silence, before Bianca turned to Raven with amusement dancing on her pretty face.

"Poking the bear, are you then?"

"It's hard not to. He's so uptight. Plus, he seems to think since he dragged me from Galway that I'm just at his beck and call. That's not really how I roll." Raven nodded to the papers in front of the women. "Can I help?"

"I like him. He took the time to show me the Alicorns yesterday. I think he's quite kind, Raven," Lily said, her voice sweet and melodious. She was an interesting contrast to the king's powerful presence, but Raven suspected she held her own quiet strength as well. If the way the king doted on her was any indication, she was the one in control in that relationship.

"That doesn't make him any less annoying," Raven muttered.

"Interesting," Bianca mused, pursing her lips, and Raven pointed a finger at her.

"Nope. Not interesting. Don't get any ideas there."

"What ideas? *Me*? Getting *ideas*? Wouldn't think of it," Bianca said cheerfully.

"She's definitely getting ideas. Bianca loves being a matchmaker," Lily added.

"Well, find someone else. I'm not a plaything for your amusement."

"Hold on then." Bianca held up a hand, tilting her head at Raven. "That's not what I'm saying. I may enjoy helping people find love, but I would never do so just for my own fun, particularly at the expense of someone else's feelings. If you're saying that's not the way of it, then I'll respect your feelings, Raven."

Raven read the truth in her eyes, and she sighed, pinching her nose. It was such an innate response, slapping people back when they danced too close to her vulnerable spots, that she did it without thinking. But she liked Bianca. And in the interest of finding some sort of allies in this crazy Fae world, it wouldn't hurt her to give this friendship thing a go.

"I'm sorry. I'm not much used to talking about these things. Matters of the heart and all that."

"Then this *is* a matter of the heart?" Bianca raised an eyebrow, clearly forgiving her. Maybe it was that easy, this friendship thing.

"I...I don't know. I can't rightly say at the moment. He intrigues me, I guess. More so than anyone else I've met. Let's just say I'm not unaffected by him. At the same time, I don't want to be affected by him either. Is that fair?"

"That's fair," Lily interjected. "He's quite gorgeous. The Fae have a powerful appeal, don't they?"

"They do." Bianca fanned her face. "Married over twenty years now and still just as excited by my man as the first days of our relationship."

"That's a fine thing, then, isn't it?" Lily beamed at Bianca, and Raven relaxed with the focus off her.

"You take your time with all of this, Raven. Just because you have a mild attraction for a hot Fae doesn't mean you have to do a damn thing about it. But if you want to, well, we're your women to talk to. Now, shall we crack on?" Bianca shifted the conversation back to the manuscripts, and Raven let out a small sigh of relief. It was nice, this girlfriend thing, even if she wasn't really sure how to navigate it. They didn't press her or force her to explain feelings that she didn't quite understand herself, and that was certainly something she appreciated.

"Yes. How can I help?"

"Translation key is here." Bianca nudged a sheet of paper toward Raven. "A lot of the old Fae manuscripts are written in their own language. It's painstaking to transcribe, so any extra eyes help."

"Sure thing. This is right up my alley. I used to spend most of my free time in the library. Particularly in the winter," Raven said, pulling the sheet of paper close so she could scan the writing. "Kept me warm."

"Not much in the way of heat at your place then?" Bianca asked, and Raven glanced up, realizing she'd revealed more than intended.

"Ah, well, it wasn't until recently that I had my own

place. And even then, electric is pricey. Nothing a good pair of wool socks and a proper jumper can't help with, right?" Raven asked.

"Oh, Raven. Did you not have a place to go to?" Lily looked at her with sympathy in her eyes, and Raven sighed. It was easy to put Bianca off, but Lily was too damn sweet to be tough with.

"I grew up on the streets. Took me a while, but I found my way. Singing saved me. I've got a good enough reputation now. Make some good money singing for my supper. Nothing to be ashamed of. Busking is a time-honored tradition, you know." Raven shrugged.

"You're a busker? Oh, they're my favorite." Lily clapped her hands together like it was Christmas morning. "Seriously, I stop and listen to every singer. It takes so much courage to just...sing. In front of everyone! I applaud you. You're really brave."

"I'm not sure it was brave so much as a necessity." Raven brushed the compliment away.

"It can be both," Bianca said, reaching over to squeeze her arm quickly. "One doesn't detract from the other."

"She's right. Will you sing for us?" Lily asked.

"Right now?" Raven laughed. "My guitar is in my room. I'd much prefer to have it."

"Then later? Or perhaps...what about a song before we leave for the battle? Something to empower the troops and all that?" Lily asked, hope on her lovely face.

"Sure, and I can do that. I do have experience in getting a crowd going," Raven agreed, blowing out a breath, relieved she wouldn't have to perform right at this moment. She'd already had a lot of firsts for today, and her feelings were a bit frayed at the edges.

"It's a deal then. One rousing battle song." Lily beamed, and Raven understood why Callum was so taken with her. When she smiled, it was like a sunflower turning to the sky.

"What kind of things am I looking for?" Raven asked as Bianca slid her a notebook.

"Rituals. Anything that mentions immortality. Or anything to do with the goddess origin story. That kind of thing," Bianca muttered. She bit on the end of a pencil and had another tucked behind her ear.

"Got it." Raven picked up the translation key, and her heart stuttered in her chest.

This was the same lettering as the inscription on her necklace.

The necklace that had never seemed to leave her.

No matter how hard she'd tried to rid herself of it.

The inscription was burned into her brain. She'd spent countless hours staring at it, tracing her fingers across the deep engraving in the pendant, and now the words came back to her as she stared in shock at the translation key. Sweat beaded her brow, and the room suddenly felt like it was closing in on her, and she needed to get up, to move, to run...something.

"Did you find something?" Lily asked, and Raven glanced up to see concern furrowed on her brow.

"No, I just...I didn't eat today. I got lightheaded for a moment."

"There's snacks over there. No food or drink near the

manuscripts though." Bianca nodded to a sideboard that held an array of food.

"Perfect, thanks." Raven wasn't hungry, not in the slightest, but at the very least it would give her a moment to collect herself. She stood and crossed the room, steadying her breathing, and poured herself a glass of water from a gold pitcher. Fancy, these Fae were. She took a moment to be amused at the fact that someone like her, who danced on the fringes of society, was now drinking from a gold cup. Once she'd finished her water, halfheartedly nibbled on a cookie, and collected herself, Raven returned to the table. This was it. The moment she'd been waiting for all her life.

Finally, a clue to her past.

The other women were silent, their pencils hurrying across their notebooks, and Raven bent her head, pulling a manuscript to her along with a fresh sheet of paper. Under the ruse of translating a script, she began to write out the inscription on her necklace, the letters blurring until they came into focus when she finished.

Bloodsong.

That was it? Raven checked her work, making sure her translation was correct, and then quickly flipped a page, surprised to find that she was near tears. Once more she pushed away from the table and crossed to the food, pouring another glass of water while she calmed her emotions. Fury and sadness whirled in her core as she tried to make sense of the inscription. Was that her last name then? Raven Bloodsong? Albeit, while a cool name, it didn't quite ring true to her. That being said, Raven had learned to not dismiss anything, so once she had a chance to get to a computer, she was going to research the name Bloodsong. It wasn't likely that the Fae had internet. While their magick was highly advanced in many areas, some basic technologies might be outdated, or even non-existent.

Bloodsong. Raven Bloodsong. It certainly had a ring to it. Maybe it was right, and that was why she was a singer. That, at least, made some sort of weird sense.

"Oh, I found something," Lily said, drawing Raven back to the table. "Look, I think they were right. This says that we could substitute something of equal magick to the amulet. See? But it has to be of equal, or even more importance, actually. What would be more important than the ruling amulet?"

"A keepsake," Raven said automatically, and Bianca glanced at her, approval in her eyes.

"She's right. Strong magick is passed down among bloodlines. Let's find Kellen and see if we can get something of meaning worthy of sacrifice."

"It will be something to do with his mother. His grief is strong," Raven offered.

"Right. Not likely the easiest thing to ask for." Bianca slid a glance at Raven, an eyebrow raised. Raven sighed.

"I'll do it."

"You're a good one, Raven. Glad to have you on the team."

14

KELLEN

RAVEN WAS silent through most of the late dinner they took in a quiet room nestled deep in the inner recesses of the cliffs, and Kellen wondered if she was scared about the impending battle. When everyone stood to retire for the evening, he silently showed her to her room.

"Rest up. We have more preparations in the morning," Kellen said.

It wasn't what he wanted to say.

He wanted to ask if he could keep her company.

If they could talk.

Watching all the other couples drift away to their rooms had struck a chord of loneliness in him. Perhaps it was more pronounced now that Alistair was gone, for they'd spent much of their free time together, racing the wind, and now Kellen felt adrift and alone without his best friend.

"Will you do the same? Rest, that is?" Raven asked,

tilting her head up as he leaned against the door. She looked impossibly lovely in the warm light of the hallway, the shadows of her cheekbones a stark contrast to her plump lips.

"No. I'm taking night watch," Kellen said. Raven's mouth dropped open.

"For the entire kingdom? Surely, you've got guards for that," Raven protested, and his heart warmed at her concern for him.

"I do. But we still need a leader up at all times. I'm the commander this evening."

"Can't they just come and wake you if there's trouble?"

"No, that's not really how it works," Kellen said, amused at her distress. "It's fine. I'm quite used to late nights." He didn't mention that grief and worry over being a good leader kept him up most evenings anyway.

"Fine, then. I'll come with you." Raven sighed and gestured for him to turn around.

"No, you won't. You'll stay here and rest. You need to sleep, Raven."

"Sleep? Please. I just slept for what felt like days. That's the most sleep I've had in years. Trust me when I say that I'm well adjusted to short hours of rest. Look at me. It's wide awake I am." Raven pointed to her face.

"You're safe here," Kellen said. "Don't you want to catch up on rest?"

"And miss all the fun? Nah." Raven waved it away and then nudged him forward with her fist. "Go on then. Show me what this night watch is all about."

"It can be quite boring."

"You can entertain me with great stories of your people."

"And you yours."

"I don't have any people." Kellen barely heard her words, as she'd muttered them under her breath, but he tucked them away in his brain for later examination.

The night air was cool, but not cold enough to warrant an extra layer, and the scent of rain hovered on the wind. Not that it ever rained here. They lived above the clouds, so weather wasn't much of a concern for the Air Fae, but it was great fun to watch a storm from above. Judging from the gentle rumbling sound that danced on the breeze, a storm was playing out below them. Suddenly, Kellen found himself wanting to share the experience with Raven.

"Ever seen a storm from above?"

"What?" Raven stopped and looked up at him in confusion.

"You know. A storm? Rain. Clouds. Lightning?" Kellen waited for her response.

"From above? No. I've never flown before. In fact, my first ever flight was...with you."

For some reason, it pleased Kellen immensely that he had given her a first.

"I can smell it. On the wind. There's a storm brewing. Because we live above the clouds, we can watch it from above."

"And we won't get wet?" Raven scrunched her nose up as she thought about it.

"No. It's like flying in one of your airplanes. We live above the clouds."

"Wait...why can I breathe here?" Raven grabbed his arm as he took off to wander down the path that led past the stables. "I don't know why I didn't think about it before. Shouldn't I be, like, gasping for air or something?"

"Magick." Kellen waved a finger in the air. "We're mostly adapted, but we have added protections in place. Particularly once our king fell in love with a human. Lily needs to be able to travel safely in any realm. We make it possible."

"Huh. That's considerate of you."

"It's just what you do. When you care." Kellen shrugged. "Come on. We'll take watch on the cliffs past the stables. It's one of the best spots to watch the storms."

Kellen looped his arm through hers, noticing that even though she stiffened at his touch, she didn't pull away. Progress, at least. Then, because he knew the path by heart, he led her along in the darkness, past the stables where some of the Alicorns played in the pasture, softly glowing in the moonlight.

"Well, shite. They glow," Raven whispered.

"Would you expect anything less?" Kellen asked, happy that she saw the Alicorns in the same way that he did. Yes, in the daylight, they were majestic beasts. But at night? When starlight danced across their coats? They shimmered and shone with a universal energy that transcended all space and time.

"I have no idea what to expect. I don't have much frame of reference for the magickal," Raven admitted.

"Come on then, you'll love this. We're almost there."

Kellen dragged her to the edge of the cliffs, scanning the night for any signs of a threat.

"Wait, wait, wait. Hold up. That's too close." Raven dug in her heels when they neared the edge of the cliffs. He'd forgotten that she couldn't fly, so she wouldn't want to sit directly on the edge like he was used to doing. More than once, a stiff breeze had toppled him off the side, and he'd ride the wind for a moment before popping back to the castle. Without the magick of the Air Fae though, Raven would plummet to the earth.

"Come this way." Kellen led her up a path where a cluster of boulders nestled together and sat, pulling her down next to him. She automatically shifted so that she didn't lean into his side, and they settled quietly with their backs against the rocks.

From here, the world seemed to just...drop away. Living above the clouds meant they had a front-row seat to the stars, and the sky stretched above them, inky velvet scattered with ice-chip diamonds. Below, the lights of earth were shrouded by a thick blanket of clouds that were barely distinguishable in the darkness. Until...

"Oh!" Raven gasped and surprised him by gripping his hand. "Oh, Kellen. Just look!"

"Beautiful, isn't it?" Kellen said.

Below them, the dark clouds illuminated with lightning, an extraordinary show. Thick streaks of light bounced between puffy cotton clouds, illuminating various corners of the sky in an elaborate display of nature's glory.

"I've never seen anything like it," Raven breathed. Turning, he studied her face, child-like in its awe, as the dim light rippled across her skin. She was impossibly lovely, here in this moment, with all of her walls dropped.

"I would come here. Every night after my mother died. Hoping to hear from her one more time," Kellen admitted. "This was where she used to find me, when I was a child, and I'd run off after an argument with my father. If I couldn't be out racing the wind, then I'd be here, clinging to the edge of the world while I tried to make sense of my emotions."

"Not a bad spot to have a think on life, I suppose." Raven shrugged, her eyes still on the storm that raged below them.

"What about you? Did you ever have a spot? A safe place to run to? I confess, I don't really understand what you mean when you say you grew up on the streets. Maybe it's getting lost in translation between our worlds." Kellen hoped she'd open up to him, as he dearly wanted to know more, and he waited in silence while she considered his question.

"I did have this one spot. It was on the river. Nobody knew about it because you had to be just small enough to slip through a fence to get down the banks. But then, when I tucked myself under the bridge, I'd be sheltered from the rain, and nobody could see me. That was my place. My spot. I would sit there for hours. Singing softly to myself. Or to the ravens. They'd come by to listen. Or I'd just watch the water drift by. Even catching some sleep. Otherwise, the library was the closest thing I had to a safe spot, I guess." Raven's words struck a chord in him, filling him with sadness, but he sensed she wasn't interested in his sympathy.

"No home then? Is that what that means? To grow up on the streets? No shelter?"

"That's right." Raven laughed, shaking her head. "I mean, I was in and out of foster homes for a bit. It wasn't a life totally lived on the streets. But I left the last foster home and never looked back."

"What's a foster home?"

"Um, just a place where kids with no family can go. They are kind of a stand-in family without being your family."

"And you didn't like the replacement family?"

"They didn't like me," Raven said, tugging on her braid, and Kellen's heart twisted a bit. Leaning closer, he bumped a shoulder to hers as the thunder rolled across the sky.

"I like you."

"What?" Raven looked up at him in shock.

"I like you."

"Oh, please. I've done nothing but poke at you since we've met. I've deliberately tried to annoy you. You don't know me well enough to like me," Raven protested. If he looked close enough, Kellen could just make out the stars reflected in her eyes.

"You're smart. You're resilient. You're tough because you've had to be, but you don't blink twice at handling difficult situations or helping others. You have moments of being funny."

"Just moments? Damn, and here I pride myself on my excellent wit." Raven snapped her fingers in disgust.

"And, despite what you say, you are an enchantress. You, Raven, are heartstoppingly, achingly beautiful. When I look at you, like this, with your guard down? I don't know that I've ever seen a more beautiful woman in all my life."

"Kellen..." Raven's mouth opened but nothing else came out as she stared at him in disbelief. *Would she let me kiss her?* He didn't want to push her, knowing how resistant she was to touch.

"I've got a powerful curiosity about you, Raven." Kellen held his hand to his heart. "Right here. I think...I think I can feel you. Inside me. Since the moment I met you, squaring off to me on the street, you've captivated me. I don't quite know what to do about these thoughts, these feelings I'm having. Any other time, well, I'd give it a go. But I'm not sure that's the right move now."

"It isn't?" Kellen's lips quirked at Raven's annoyed tone. Perhaps she *was* equally as interested as he was.

"There are several factors at play here, Raven. The biggest being...we're leaving for a battle. I still don't know why the Domnua are hunting you. Will it be harder to protect you if I grow more attached to you? Not to mention the fact that you're as skittish as a baby Alicorn. I wouldn't feel comfortable touching you, at least not without your permission."

"Oh," Raven said, and he watched a mixture of emotions play out across her face. Silence fell, and Kellen allowed it, not needing to push her into anything she wasn't ready for. Hell, he didn't even know what *he* was ready for. His emotions were pulled in every direction as it was, and Raven entering the picture had been an unexpected distraction for him. "What a strange conversation we're having. I've never had anyone look at me the way that you do, or see me the way that you have. Nobody's...

taken care with me before. Not like this. I'm curious as well." Raven said the last bit on a rush of breath, like she was scared she wouldn't say the words if she didn't get them out quickly.

"What are you curious about, exactly?" Kellen held his breath, waiting for her response.

"About you. About...why I think about you too. I think...well, I mean, obviously you're attractive." Raven shrugged.

"Thank you, that's very kind of you to say," Kellen said, amused as she muddled her way through her thoughts.

"So it's normal I would be attracted to you, right? I'm sure every woman would be. That's probably all this is, then. Just the whole...proximity to a hot guy thing. It doesn't happen all that often for me. It's normal for me to be interested. Right?"

"I can't speak to that other than no, I don't think that every woman finds me attractive." Though many did, but Kellen suspected Raven wouldn't be interested in hearing about his past. Just because he'd never sought to find his fated mate, didn't mean that he hadn't enjoyed his time with women. The Fae were a lustful bunch, and that was the truth of it.

"Maybe it's just like, an itch to be scratched," Raven mused, and Kellen's eyebrows shot up. This was the first time he'd heard of lovemaking described in such a manner.

"Maybe," Kellen agreed, keeping his tone serious.

"Because it can't really be anything more, anyway. You live here. I live down there. I guess this would be, what, a vacation fling? You know, how people go on holiday and hook up for the weekend?" Raven looked up at him, and Kellen honestly had no idea what she was babbling on about.

"I don't understand what a fling is."

"Oh, it's like...a short-term romance. A one-night stand. A no-attachments, mutual, pleasure-sharing thing."

"Mutual pleasure sharing," Kellen repeated, working hard now not to laugh. Raven was beyond adorable as she worked herself around to trying to give herself permission to kiss him. He needed to wait her out, but since she was already thinking about it, he suspected it wouldn't be long now. Patience would win in the end. "Is that what you like?"

"I can't say. I've never tried it." Raven looked him up and down, like he was a new toy to buy at the market.

"Raven." Kellen leaned forward, desperately trying not to laugh. "Just tell me what you want."

"I can't just say it." Raven threw up her hands, exasperated.

"Surely, you can. It's just you and me here. In the dark. Hanging on the edge of the world overlooking a storm. Your secret is safe with me."

"I want to kiss you," Raven blurted out. "But I don't know if I'll be good at it, and I'm worried that I'll screw it up."

Ah. It made more sense now. She was inexperienced, which contributed to her nerves. Still, he didn't reach for her.

"You can't screw it up. That's just not possible." Kellen leaned back against the bolder and looked up at the stars.

"*Of course* it's possible. I hear people talking about bad kissers all the time."

"Just take your time with it. I promise you'll enjoy it."

"Me?" Raven squeaked. "You want me to kiss you?"

"I gather that you like being in control. Wouldn't it be easier for you to take the lead? More comfortable?" Kellen just tilted his head to look at her, keeping his shoulders against the rock behind him. No sudden movements.

"Right, well, hmmm," Raven murmured under her breath as she looked at him. "Just like do it then? Like no buildup or anything?"

"Would you like poetry, my little nightbird?"

"Nightbird?" Raven cocked an eyebrow at him.

"Raven. Your name. Bird of the night, flying amongst the stars, enchanting my soul."

"Oh, you're good at this. Right, well, then, let's get on with it." Raven leaned forward and pressed her lips firmly against his, and Kellen's heart leapt, even though he was amused at her determination. He understood what it took to be brave, so instead, he waited, opening his lips just a bit and angling his head in encouragement.

"There. How was that?" Raven broke the kiss.

"Delightful," Kellen said. He lifted his hands. "May I? Sometimes it helps if you can touch."

"Touch where?" Raven demanded, narrowing her eyes.

"Here." Kellen reached out and lightly danced his

fingers across her neck. "And sometimes here." He traced a hand over her shoulder.

"That might be fine then," Raven agreed, suspicion lacing her tone.

"We'll take it slow," Kellen promised. Turning, so he faced her, Kellen ran his thumb lightly across her lip, heat building in him as her lips parted. She looked both nervous and trusting, and it made him feel both powerful and protective of her. Trailing his hand down the side of her neck, he brushed his finger across the back of her head and gently angled her face for a kiss. Leaning down, Kellen brushed his lips lightly across hers, once, twice, three times, before lingering over her lips.

She tasted like moondust and honey.

Kellen drew the moment out, caressing his lips over hers, nibbling lightly, before gently running his tongue across her lower lip. At her gasp of excitement, he took the opening she offered, and dipped his tongue inside, licking softly into her mouth as she moaned in pleasure. Kellen lingered there, enjoying the give and take of the kiss, allowing Raven to explore in her own right. When her hands came up to thread through his hair, he shifted ever so slightly to pull her closer to him.

Raven broke the kiss.

"What are you doing?"

"I believe it's called a hug in your culture. I suppose I would say I'm...cradling you in my arms?" Kellen raised a brow.

"Why?"

"Because it feels nice." Kellen laughed.

"I guess it does." Raven sounded suspicious of a hug,

and he took a moment, burying his face in her hair, while his heart hammered in his chest over this impossible contradiction of a woman.

"Can I tell you what I'd like to do right now?"

"If it's butt stuff, I'm out of here."

"What? No." Kellen laughed outright. "That's quite a leap you make there, Nightbird. I want to pull you onto my lap, put my arms around you, and hold you close while we watch the storm. Would that be okay with you?"

"And that's it? You just want to hold me?" Raven looked up at him, concern in her eyes. "Was I a bad kisser then?"

"No. Raven, no. You're a wonderful kisser. But if we keep kissing like that I'm going to want to kiss you everywhere. I'll want to kiss you until all thoughts leave that busy brain of yours, and all you can do is feel, and then when pleasure comes, it's my name at your lips."

"Oh..." Raven's eyes grew wide. "That doesn't sound awful."

"It's not. I promise you it's not. But it's too much for you right now. We'll get there. If you want to. But in your own time. For now, let's try a hug."

With that, Raven allowed him to pull her onto his lap. He cradled her against his chest, his lips at her ear, and together, two lost souls, they watched the storm play out below them.

15

RAVEN

"WHEN SHE SINGS, queens will fall, daughters by blood, end them all."

Lily blinked at Bianca and Raven who stared at her across the table. They were back in the library the next morning, using every possible moment to try and find any hidden gems that might help their ritual. A chill crept across Raven's skin at Lily's words. It sounded so... epic. Final. Catastrophic. Maybe this was the end of the world, after all, and Raven was just slow to catch up. Granted, it had only been a matter of days since she'd arrived in the Fae realm, while the others had been fighting these battles for years.

"Ladies." Seamus poked his head in the door with a grin. "You are formally invited to Alicorn racing training."

"No way!" Lily exclaimed, jumping up and clapping her hands in delight. "We get to ride them ourselves?"

"It occurred to us that you may be called upon to ride

one of these beautiful creatures. Particularly if we fly them into battle. While the Alicorns are quite adept at keeping riders on their back, it's best if you have at least one ride under your belt."

"You're taking the Alicorns to battle?" Raven's stomach dropped. An image of the chubby alicorns playing in the field popped in her head, and she worried they'd be left without their family to look over them.

"Some, yes. It's their choice," Seamus said, understanding crossing his face as Bianca went to him and wrapped her arms around his waist. "Kellen has promised me that they are in control. If they don't want to go, they are free to stay here under the protection of the royal guard."

"Of course they want to go. They're just full of bravery and light, aren't they?" Bianca sighed. "I've seen a lot of cool things since I've come to the Fae realm, but the Alicorns might very well be my favorite."

"Did you know they glow at night?" Raven asked, stretching her arms above her head to work out the tension in her shoulders. Today she wore the same buttery-soft leather pants, but her jumper was a soft muted grey that matched her eyes.

"How do you know that?" Bianca asked, tilting her head at Raven in question. "I thought we weren't allowed in the stables at night."

"Kellen took me." Raven said the words without thinking and then realized her mistake when Bianca shooed Seamus from the room, and the two women cornered her.

"Tell us everything," Bianca demanded. "Leave nothing out. *Nothing.*"

"Unless you want to, of course," Lily added.

"What? We just…" Heat bloomed on Raven's cheeks, and she ducked her head, but not before Bianca's eagle eyes caught it.

"Something happened! Oh, I'm dying to know."

"She doesn't have to tell us anything," Lily persisted.

"I know, I know. But if she felt like telling us, she could. Or even throwing us a wee tidbit, surely that would be what friends do?" Bianca wheedled, and Raven laughed. She *did* want to tell them. She'd been bursting with the news all morning, barely having slept that morning when they'd returned to the castle after a quiet night on the cliffs. All she knew was that she wanted to kiss Kellen again and needed to work up the courage to ask him for it. Or maybe she'd just do it. Surprise him with a kiss. But that would be bad, wouldn't it? She didn't like it when people forced affection on her. She'd better be respectful of his space then too. Raven worried her lower lip as she thought about it.

"We kissed," Raven said, finally, and both women cheered.

"I knew it. I called it, didn't I?" Bianca all but preened, pumping a fist in the air. "I've got a good eye for these things."

"How was it?" Lily asked, reaching out to squeeze her hand. "Are you happy about it?"

"It was…" Raven brought a hand to her lips, as though she could still feel the kiss. Her first *real* kiss. "Wonderful. Like…I don't even have words. I just…"

"Told ya," Bianca nodded knowingly. "The Fae. They know what they're doing."

"He said he likes me," Raven rushed out, holding her hands up helplessly. Again, Raven considered Kellen's words from the night before. *"You, Raven, are heartstoppingly, achingly beautiful. When I look at you, like this, with your guard down? I don't know that I've ever seen a more beautiful woman in all my life."* The words had stunned her then, and they were stunning her now. "What am I supposed to do about that?"

"*Awww.*" Bianca fanned her face.

"What do you want to do about it?" Lily asked, concern furrowing her brow.

"I don't know. I like him too. I think. I guess I want to spend more time with him?"

"Then that's all you need to do. Nothing needs to be decided today," Bianca advised. "We've got Alicorns to ride. Battles to be won. Rituals to be enacted. Somewhere, in all that, I suspect the two of you will sort yourselves out."

"You'll find a path together," Lily promised.

"Or not," Bianca added, and Lily glared at her. Bianca laughed. "What? Raven needs to know it will be okay whatever choice she makes. Date the hot Fae ruler. Don't date the hot Fae ruler. Either way, we'll be here to listen."

Raven looked between the two women who had very quickly become the closest thing she'd had to friends. *No, they* are *my friends.* She was allowed to have friendships with people. These two wouldn't drop her at a moment's notice.

"Thank you. Truly. It means a lot to me," Raven

admitted, feeling a weird knot form in her chest like she wanted to cry. But she wasn't much for crying, as it never solved anything, so instead she just stood there with her hand at her chest and looked helplessly at the two women.

"Shall we go ride some Alicorns?" Bianca asked, seeming to understand that Raven was incapable of communicating her feelings in that moment.

"Did you see the babies? They're super chubby, feisty little things."

Lily sucked in a breath.

"Chubby Alicorn babies?"

"Indeed."

"I'm dead. I've died and gone to heaven."

They chattered about the Alicorn babies all the way to the stables where they found Kellen and Callum standing in the pasture with several Alicorns milling about.

"Just look at this handsome lot." Bianca grinned at the men. "Pretty as a picture you are."

"Why is everyone calling me pretty all the time?" Kellen groused, but his eyes were on Raven. She hadn't seen him since they'd parted in the early hours of the morning, and a shiver danced across her skin at his look. Awareness filled her, making her limbs feel heavy, and heat pooled low in her gut. Was this what wanting a man was like? No wonder people got in such a fuss over sex all the time. She was reminded of her ride from Galway, pressed tightly between his muscular thighs, and how his size easily dwarfed hers. She was still strong, Raven reminded herself, as they crossed the pasture. Riker trotted forward, letting out a soft whinny of delight, and a wide grin split her face. It was silly, really, to be this excited that an animal remembered her. Was this how people with pets felt? And, yet. Riker was more than just an animal, wasn't he?

"Hi, friend," Raven whispered softly to him, stroking the side of his neck. Look at her adding all these new friends to her roster. She positively didn't recognize herself. Who knew that personal growth had only been one Fae realm away?

An image of her riding Riker while he shot fire from his horn flashed into Raven's head.

"I don't know if I want you to go into battle, Riker. I'm worried about you," Raven whispered, as she pressed her forehead to the side of his neck. "What if you get hurt? Shouldn't you stay here? Protect the babies?"

Riker stomped a hoof, and Raven took that to mean he disagreed with her.

"He wants to go," Kellen said from behind her, the warm timbre of his voice sending a thrill of excitement down her body. Raven was unaccountably nervous, not wanting to turn around and look at him. What if he regretted their kiss? Then, annoyed at herself with such silly thoughts when they were in the middle of training for a battle, she forced herself to turn.

"That is what he seems to be telling me. I worry for them." Raven took a deep breath for courage and finished her thought. Being vulnerable took more guts than she'd realized. "And for you, Kellen."

"Ah, Raven." Kellen stepped forward, a smile hovering at his lips, and he reached out to touch her, pausing mid-air before he did. He paid attention, Raven realized. He'd known that she was uncomfortable being close to people, and even now, after they'd cuddled all night, he waited for her permission. *Screw it.* She stepped forward and wrapped her arms around Kellen's waist like she'd seen Bianca do with Seamus. It had looked so lovely and sweet, and she'd realized that maybe she wanted something like that too. A surprised laugh came from Kellen's chest. She could hear it rumble through him. "I'll be just fine. It's you I'm worried about. Well, you and the other women. Try as I might, I couldn't convince the men to tell them to stay home."

Kellen's arms tightened around her, and they stood like that for a moment, with Riker making a happy humming noise behind them.

"I think he's happy with us hugging," Raven said, eyeing the Alicorn.

"He's never liked that I'm lonely. The Alicorns are herd animals. Riker seems to think I need my own herd."

"Are you lonely?" Raven looked up, caught on his words. She'd always been lonely, but it had morphed over the years from loneliness to a staunch sense of independence.

"More so now that Alistair is gone. It's not easy making friends as a leader."

More than anything, Raven could understand the stark sense of loss that came when people left. Be it through death or choice, a loss was a loss. It was funny how she was already feeling a touch protective of him. She tightened her arms around his waist for a big squeeze, before forcing herself to step back. Feelings of guilt momentarily raced through her. She'd stolen Alistair's coin, something that she normally wouldn't worry about. She had to live. But now she knew of the man as someone's friend, and that bit at her conscience. When the time was right, she'd return it to Kellen. There wasn't much she could do about Alistair being gone, but she would do everything in her power to prepare for this upcoming battle so Kellen didn't experience more loss. Was that the way of it when people liked each other?

"Let's fly!" Bianca crowed, drawing Raven's attention away from Kellen, and she looked up to see her already mounted on an Alicorn.

"Looking good up there," Raven called. It wasn't a lie either. Bianca looked fierce on the back of the Alicorn, which gamely spread its wings and bowed its head lightly, while Bianca held one fist in the air.

"I'm going to have a painting made of you like this," Seamus said. "Is it bad that I'm turned on right now?"

"I'd expect nothing less." Bianca blew him a kiss.

"Let's get you up there before this turns into foreplay." Kellen cupped his hands and crouched.

"What are you doing?" Raven narrowed her eyes at him.

"Put your foot in my hand. I'm helping you up."

"Oh, right." She did as he asked, and in moments she was settled astride Riker. "Do I need a saddle or like a halter or something? How am I not going to fall off?"

It had been one thing to ride an Alicorn when Kellen was holding her tightly, but now, when she was on her own? Nerves kicked in, causing her stomach to twist.

A picture of a waterfall popped into her head.

"Why is he sending me waterfall images?" Raven asked, her stomach twisting even more as Riker shifted lightly beneath her. Her world swayed, as she adjusted to being on the back of a massive animal.

"That's his calming image. It's one of his favorite places to visit. It's just his attempt to soothe you."

Riker was trying to take care of her? Her heart melted into one goopy puddle in her chest.

Kellen reached up and took her hand, threading it into Riker's mane.

"Hold here. Then, clench your thighs."

At his order, Raven clenched, and a deliciously dirty image shot through her mind. Knowing Riker could pick up on thoughts, she shoved that away and focused on Kellen's words.

"If you slip, feel scared, uncertain...anything of that nature, tell Riker. He'll adjust to you. Even if you fall? He'll catch you. But he won't let you fall. And I'll be right by your side."

"Right. So hold tight and...how do I steer?"

"You don't. You just ask Riker to take you where you want to go. One thing about Alicorns? They do what they want. If he decides he doesn't want to go there—for whatever reason that may be—you'll have to trust him. He's in charge. But you're his partner. Got it?"

"Oh, right. So I don't have to like, order him around and stuff?"

"You can try it." Kellen laughed softly running his hand down Riker's flank. "He'll not likely listen."

"That's fine. He knows more about this world than I do. I'll trust his judgment."

"Ready to fly then?"

"I don't actually know how to answer that?" Raven's sentence ended in a squeak as Riker made the decision for her, flapping his large wings and taking off from the ground with just a few running steps. Raven closed her eyes and gripped his mane, clenching her legs around his muscular body as hard as she could, as she broke out into sweat.

"Breathe," Kellen shouted from somewhere next to her, and her stomach twisted as Riker dipped in the air.

"I am breathing," Raven cried.

"Open your eyes."

"I can't," Raven said, trying to count her breaths as the wind danced across her cheeks.

"You can." Kellen sounded much closer now. Taking a deep breath, Raven pried one eye open and then the other. Her world tilted as she could just make out Ireland far below them, and panic rose. She slid lightly across Riker's back, twisting, suddenly wanting nothing more than to be back on land. The waterfall image appeared in her head again, and Riker slowed, until they all but hovered in the air, while Raven adjusted her seat. "Take a moment. Don't look down. Look forward. At the horizon."

"How do you get used to this?" Raven muttered. She wanted so desperately to love this, but now, when she was on her own, fear gripped her.

"We learn at a young age."

"I don't think I can do this."

"Raven. Darling. You already are."

Raven realized that Kellen was right. Riker had picked

up speed after she'd adjusted her grip, and they cruised smoothly through the sky. Kellen was also correct about where to focus. If she kept her eyes on the horizon, it actually wasn't so bad.

"Woohoooooo!" Bianca shrieked, speeding past her with her blonde hair flowing behind her, Seamus hot on her heels. "Come on, Raven! Try and catch me."

"Oh, it's a race she's wanting?" Raven glowered, her competitive spirit edging out some of the fear.

"Are you going to let her win?" Kellen asked, his own Alicorn keeping easy pace with Riker. Raven took a deep breath and rolled her shoulders, letting the tension drain, as Lily and Callum flew in circles around them. The sun lowered in the sky, casting the moment in warm gold, like a sepia-toned photograph of olden times, and Raven wanted to capture this memory in her mind forever.

Her first real friends. Her first kiss.

And flying freakin' Alicorns.

If everything ended tomorrow, and she had to go back to living in her little studio, she'd clutch this memory to her heart for the rest of her days.

"Let's ride," Raven declared, a smile at her lips. And when Riker leapt forward, slicing through the air, she could no longer contain her own scream of excitement either. "Woooohooo!"

16

RAVEN

"WE CAN CALL IT A DRAW," Bianca offered, and Raven chuckled, sliding from Riker's back into Kellen's waiting arms. It took a moment to steady herself on the ground, and she wondered if that was what people who lived on a boat felt like when they went back to land.

"I don't think so. I'm pretty sure I won," Raven said. Kellen drew a bottle from his pocket and poured a few drops into his hand, holding it out in front of Riker's mouth. "What are you giving him?"

"Extra protection. It supercharges their healing process in case they do get wounded for any reason. It takes a few hours to settle in and work through the system, so I want to make sure they have it before we leave in the morning," Kellen explained as he went on to the next Alicorn. It was the bottle that he had taken from the weapons room, Raven realized. What other magicks could they take with them into battle tomorrow?

Into the Dark Realm.

Everyone spoke of the underworld in hushed tones, and Raven hadn't really gotten a grasp on what they were dealing with yet. She made a note to ask Kellen or Bianca later, but for now, she didn't want to think of dark realms or battles. Looping an arm over Riker's back, Raven leaned in and pressed her lips to his coat.

"Thank you for giving me that joy. It's a freedom I've never known, and I felt, I don't know, powerful up there. So, thank you, friend."

Riker stomped a hoof, leaning into her, and Raven smiled. An image of herself, hair streaming in the wind and pure joy on her face, popped into her head, and Raven hugged Riker.

They waited until Kellen had finished giving the Alicorns their special tonic, and together they walked back toward the castle. There was meant to be a rally of sorts that evening, to unite the people before half the Air Fae left for battle the next morning, and Kellen had asked her if she would sing. Normally, she enjoyed singing for a crowd, but now nerves kicked low in her gut. Would it be possible for her to perform for the Fae in the same manner that she did for people passing by on the street? In Galway, she hoped to entertain, maybe get a smile or a coin from someone passing by. But tonight? These people might lose their loved ones in the morning. How was she supposed to sing a song that would embolden them when they faced potential loss?

"Did you ask him?" Bianca dropped back, distracting Raven from her thoughts.

"Ask him what?" Confusion rippled through her.

"For a talisman. Something that could replace the amulet."

"Oh, right. I forgot, actually." Raven winced.

"We'll need it tonight, if possible. I think we're meant to charm it and put intention into the item and all that. Do you want me to ask him?"

"No, no, I can ask Kellen, it's fine."

"Ask me what?" Kellen asked, coming up behind them, and Raven winced again. Now it sounded like she'd been talking about him. She had, but not like that. Raven sighed, annoyed with herself, and turned to Kellen as Bianca made herself scarce. He looked relaxed, much more at ease than she'd seen him in days, and she realized that he'd needed to ride the wind as much as the others had. Though it had been fun, and even miraculous in its own right, it had also been a team building of sorts. A unification of their shared goals.

"Um, well. So." Raven dug her fingernails into her palms as she thought about what to ask him for.

"Just say it, Raven."

"If we want to complete the ritual, Bianca is certain we can likely be equally effective if you can substitute a different item for the amulet. Something deeply meaningful to you. I was thinking...maybe something of your mother's?" Raven trailed off at the stricken look that crossed his face. She hated being the one to remind him that his best friend had betrayed him.

"I have my mother's ring. We can use that," Kellen said, his voice stiff. Raven jerked her hand forward, and then back, and then forward again, taking his hand in her own. Once more, that little jolt of energy that seemed to bounce between them ran up her arm.

"I'm sorry, Kellen." There was nothing else she could say.

"It's just things. None of it matters if we can stop Domnu from destroying our world." Kellen shrugged. "What does Bianca need?"

"They need to lay some sort of spell on it tonight. The others are meant to arrive in the morning, and I think they're hoping to do the ritual in the Dark Realm."

"Or here, even." Bianca dropped back, having shame-lessly eavesdropped. "I was thinking there's nothing that indicates we have to do the ritual on her turf. Maybe we give it a go before we leave for battle and, who knows, perhaps we don't have to ride into darkness."

"I like that idea very much," Kellen admitted. "I'll collect her ring now."

They'd arrived at the main square where the Air Fae milled about with varying degrees of emotion on their faces. They were all lovely, Raven realized, studying the crowd as people shifted between worry and bravado. Her eyes landed on Devlin. Well, at least most of them were lovely. She still didn't like Kellen's father, not that she'd made any effort to get to know him more. Living life on the fringe had taught her to read people quickly, and Devlin just wasn't a man she was interested in interacting with.

By the time Kellen returned, a grim look on his face, her guitar at his back, the square had filled with people and Raven's nerves were tapdancing their way through her gut. *Maybe this wasn't really my place to perform.* She began edging backward. But King Callum stepped forward and raised his hands to speak.

"My mother's ring," Kellen said, his voice low, as he dropped a gold band into Bianca's hand. Immediately, she tucked it away, and then surprised Kellen by giving him a fierce hug.

"Since she's not here to hug you, I will," Bianca said, and Raven had to look away from the tender moment, her eyes threatening to mist over. She blinked rapidly, needing to push her emotions down, or she'd never be able to perform. Callum's speech faded into the background as Raven tried to calm herself.

In under a week, her life had changed dramatically. With that came a whole slew of new emotions she was unfamiliar with navigating, let alone the new relationships she'd formed. Was this the way of battles and warzones? Friendships were formed fast when tomorrow wasn't promised? Love...Raven shut down the thought that struggled to surface, wanting to claw its way out of her chest. Not love. Just affection. Good old-fashioned lust, even. But not love. Raven wasn't even sure she was capable of feeling love.

"Raven?"

Raven blinked up at the king, realizing that he'd spoken her name twice.

"Oh, right." It was now or never.

Kellen handed Raven her guitar and she walked across the square toward a small platform. Two large pillars bookended the platform, torches burning brightly at the top. Fire ringed the battlement walls that surrounded the square, the golden light mirroring the setting sun from earlier, and Raven stepped nervously onto the stage. Luckily, the Fae were much more polite than an unruly street crowd, and nobody shouted at her while she took her time tuning her guitar and gathering her thoughts.

None of her busking staples were appropriate for this moment, Raven realized, and she paused, nerves tightening her throat. Desperate, she looked to where Kellen stood, Bianca and Lily on either side of him, all three smiling at her with encouragement. But it was a small nod from Kellen, as though promising her she couldn't fail, much like the night before, that shook her out of her nerves.

If she was going to sing, well it would be from her heart.

Closing her eyes, Raven inhaled, and strummed a few chords, until her brain landed on the threads of a song. It was a song that often haunted her in her dreams, teasing her when she hovered between waking and sleep, and she reached for that melody now. Humming a bit, she allowed it to form, luminous and bright in her mind, until she could see the words flowing toward her like a waterfall cascading across the rocks.

WHERE THE SUN breaks the sky,
    Look for me in the light,
    Darling, don't you cry,
    We still have, we still have this night.

· · ·

DANCE ON THE WIND,
   for tomorrow is only a wish,
   Dance on the wind,
   This moment starts with a kiss,
   Dance on the wind,
   Our magick, our magick lies in our bliss.

RAVEN CAUGHT movement in the crowd, Kellen drawing forward as she sang, and her eyes locked on his, the flames dancing between them.

TWO LOST SOULS, caught in a breeze,
   Coming together with the greatest of ease,
   Lost to the whims of fate,
   Their hearts, their hearts will always wait.

DANCE ON THE WIND,
   Lest we forget what is right,
   Dance on the wind,
   We side, we side, with the light,
   Dance on the wind,
   For tomorrow, tomorrow we fight.

APPLAUSE BROKE OUT, but it faded into the background, a muffled roar as Kellen strode forward. The knot that had been sitting in her chest all day broke open when Kellen leapt onto the stage and lifted her into his arms. Without another word, he jumped off the stage and strode into a tunnel, leaving the cheering crowd behind him. It was so unlike him to manhandle her in such a way that Raven was torn between shock and arousal. Her heart fluttered in her chest as he carried her as though she weighed nothing, her guitar caught awkwardly between them. She studied the sharp edges of his face, set in hard lines. His expression was hard to read. Was he angry with her?

Kellen kicked his door open, causing Raven to gasp in his arms, and go on alert. This was not a man who had been charmed by her song. Perhaps her music had been wrong for his people? The door shut behind them and Kellen whisked a hand out, lighting the room with magick, and walked forward to drop her onto his bed. She shrank back, certain now that he was angry with her, and quickly divested herself of her guitar. Laying it next to her on the mattress, she met his eyes.

"Not a fan, eh?" Raven affected lightness.

"Where did you learn that song?" Kellen bit each word out, like they were being torn from his body, and she blanched.

"Learn? I didn't learn it. That's *my* song."

"It is not your song," Kellen turned to her, his eyes heated. "I'll ask you once more. Who taught you that song?"

"Nobody...I...Kellen." Raven rose, feeling at a disadvantage while seated, and anger licked tendrils at her core. "That's my song. I wrote it. Well, it comes to me in my dreams. I just...pulled it from my mind."

"In your dreams. I thought you didn't dream, Raven."

"I mean, not metaphorically speaking when I'm

thinking about my future. But in my sleep? Yes, I dream. Why are you so upset, Kellen? Please tell me, so I know what I did wrong." It wasn't in Raven's nature to ask nicely, not when faced with someone who appeared to be this angry with her, but she needed to understand more clearly what she was dealing with here.

"It's my heartsong, Raven." Kellen looked at her, and waited, as though she was supposed to know what the hell that meant. When she just shook her head at him in confusion, he leaned forward so that their faces were inches apart.

"You're my fated mate."

17

KELLEN

WHEN SHE'D STARTED to sing, Kellen's heart had broken open, a shimmering lovely liquid energy pouring through him, and he couldn't think, couldn't speak. All he could focus on was getting to her. It didn't matter to him what it looked like to his people or what his father thought. He'd just needed to get to her.

Her.

Raven.

His fated mate.

He'd heard talk of what this bond could do to a Fae. For some, it almost drove them to the brink of madness. He'd always found that suspect, but now, having heard his heartsong, Kellen understood.

He'd die for her.

He'd fight for her.

He'd do anything for her.

So long as she stayed by his side. He needed her in

this moment as much as he needed water to live, and it took every last inch of his willpower not to push her back onto the bed and claim her over and over until she understood in every cell of her being that she was his.

And he was hers.

Always. Forever on.

Whatever it took.

This bond, this knowing, was so instantaneous that even Kellen was shocked by the emotions that rampaged through him.

"Listen," Raven said, holding her hands in the air, panic skittering across her face. "I get it. It's an emotional night, a moving song, tomorrow we ride into the unknown. That's all this is, Kellen. Our emotions are running high because of what we face tomorrow. It's making us want more...think..." Raven cut herself off and waved a hand helplessly.

"Think what, Raven?" Kellen prowled closer, itching to touch her. He wondered if she knew what she'd revealed to him. Even though she might not be ready to admit it, she felt something for him.

"Just...you know. Sexy thoughts. And stuff." Raven stumbled over her words, a faint flush crossing her lovely skin.

"Are you having sexy thoughts about me then, darling?" Kellen reached up and ran a thumb lightly across her lower lip, his focus narrowing as her eyes widened at his touch. Her breath shuddered.

"I mean, yes. But it's just normal. We kissed. And you know, cuddled. And big fights, battles, emotions running high. Really, it's just a chemical response. Adrenaline. All that," Raven babbled, and Kellen lowered his head until his lips hovered close to hers.

"Tell me, nightbird, how you can sing of fate and love but not believe it for yourself?"

"Oh," Raven said, stricken, her eyes searching his. "It's just a song, Kellen."

"Words matter."

"It's...weaving a tale. A moment. That's all..." Raven trailed off when Kellen made a small noise with his mouth.

"You insult us both."

"Kellen. I think you're just caught up in—"

Raven gasped.

Gripping her waist, Kellen lifted her and rolled with her onto the bed so that she straddled him. *I'm out of patience now. I've found my mate.* As much as he wanted to cover her, to claim her, Kellen still understood that Raven needed to retain some semblance of control. She gaped down at him, surprise wreathing her face, as her slender legs straddled his thighs. Already he was achingly hard for her, and he lifted his hips, moving beneath her, and watched her eyes widen in shock.

"Does this feel like I'm just caught up in the moment?"

"Possibly?" Raven squeaked as Kellen began to move, undulating his hips beneath her, rubbing himself against the tender spot between her thighs. "It's hard to say, really."

"Will you give yourself to me, Raven darling? On this night, this eve of our greatest battle, will you let me have you?" Kellen was beyond sweet words, his desire so desperate that he just needed to be buried deep inside her. If she wasn't ready to accept that she was his fated mate, that was fine. He'd take his time convincing her. But for now, he was fairly certain he'd die if he didn't ride to battle with the taste of her on his lips.

"I...oh..." Raven's mouth rounded as he gripped her hips, holding her tight at his waist as he moved between her legs. "Kellen...I..."

"Tell me," Kellen bit out, barely able to restrain himself, as he waited for her to say whatever thoughts weighed her down.

"I've never done this before," Raven rushed out, her cheeks pinkening. At her words, Kellen stilled.

A gift.

She was a gift to him.

All his. No one before and no one after would touch her. Blood roared in his ears, and he had to force himself to take deep breaths. Though he wanted to ravish her, now was the time to take care.

"Will you share yourself with me?" Kellen asked, his eyes heavy on hers. The moment drew out until finally, finally, Raven nodded. Kellen closed his eyes, relief pouring through him, before he lifted her and rolled, reversing their positions.

"Um, it's just..." Raven began and Kellen laughed, covering her mouth with his own. By the time he'd kissed her breathless, she was panting beneath his lips, her hips rocking gently toward his.

"Raven. Darling?"

"Yes?"

"Unless it's telling me how to pleasure you, you're not allowed to talk."

"Oh. Is it abnormal to talk during sex?" Raven asked and then grimaced when Kellen gave her a look. "Right. Got it. I'll be quiet."

"You're wearing much too many clothes." Kellen snapped his fingers and Raven screeched, holding her hands across her now naked body.

"What the hell?"

"This is how I prefer you. Remember the first morning that I came to wake you? You were half naked in bed. I've been thinking of that moment since," Kellen said, having removed his own clothes as well. He ran a hand down her side, watching how she shivered under his touch. "I want to go slow with you. I want to savor you, like the most succulent of fruits on a hot summer's day, but I fear I won't be able to control myself." He bent forward, capturing her lips once more, and she hummed against his mouth, arching her body toward his.

"Um, that's fine. You can just...do what you have to do," Raven said.

Kellen paused, and then threw his head back and laughed.

"Oh, nightbird, I plan to. I think, based on that busy brain of yours and the nerves I can see all but dancing across your skin, that I best make you forget to think."

"Um, sure I guess..." Raven gasped as Kellen danced his fingers up the tender flesh of her thigh.

"Here's what I'm going to do, Raven. I've a powerful thirst for you. I want to lick every inch of your body, tasting you, and discovering just where you're most sensitive. But already, I can tell that will have to wait until after. You're curious, aren't you, what it feels like...to be worshipped this way?" Kellen traced his finger between her legs and Raven jolted at his touch. "Have you touched yourself here?"

"Sometimes," Raven admitted, her voice breathy.

"Tell me what you like, Raven. Do you like when I touch you like this?" Gently, Kellen opened her, finding her already slick with desire, and he buried his face at her neck, kissing gently as he explored. Raven bucked under his hands, whimpering as he found her most sensitive spot, and he stayed there, circling tirelessly, until she cried out.

"I'm going to..."

"Release, my love. Release. I want you to seek your pleasure at my touch," Kellen said, rolling to kiss her as she cried out into his mouth, riding his hand. When she collapsed back, her eyes wide, Kellen grinned.

"Maybe I do have a touch more control than I thought. I fear I may need to take more time with you than anticipated. Now that I know just how beautifully you come."

Raven's cheeks flushed, and she opened her mouth.

He pinched her nipple to distract her, and she glared at him.

"No talking. Don't overthink. Just feel."

With that, Kellen kissed his way down her body, noting how she arched her breasts into his mouth when he captured a nipple with his lips, and how she shivered when he lingered over the soft skin of her thighs.

"I'm dying to taste you, sweet Nightbird," Kellen bit softly, and her legs jerked. "Will you let me kiss you?"

"Down there?" Raven squeaked. Her body jerked once more when he traced a finger lightly across her folds.

"Yes, unless you had another place you were interested in me touching? Your feet, perhaps?" Kellen laughed into her thigh when she jerked her foot away from his nearest wandering hand.

"No. No. Not my feet. Um, so you'll just...like..."

"Why don't I show you?" Kellen waited a beat and when she didn't stop him, he brought his mouth to the apex of her thighs, tasting her sweetness as her hips jerked involuntarily against his face.

"Holy...shite," Raven moaned, "Kellen...I need..."

Taking the invitation, Kellen reached beneath Raven and cupped her bum with his hands, lifting her to give him unfettered access, and he proceeded to feast. Raven's back arched, as she pressed herself against him, and he couldn't help but love how her legs shook when he tasted her slick heat with his tongue. Finally, finally, when she'd cried out once more, trembling against his mouth, Kellen shifted to move himself back up her body.

A soft pink flush covered her delicate skin, and her eyes were drowsy with lust, her mouth slightly swollen from his kisses. Never had he seen a more beautiful woman.

"Well. I quite enjoyed that," Raven admitted, and Kellen fell straight off the cliff into love for this bristly, yet vulnerable woman.

Kellen angled himself between her legs, a smile hovering at his lips, as love filled him.

"Raven, look at me," Kellen ordered, nudging her gently with his hard length. Raven lifted her eyes, heavy with lust. "You might not be ready to hear this, but I'll say it anyway. I claim you. My fated mate, my heart, my everything."

Raven's mouth dropped open, and he leaned forward, his lips gentle on hers as he entered her in one strong motion, her body adjusting to accommodate him. At her sharp inhalation, he paused, waiting, while his body screamed with delight about being buried deep inside his fated mate. This woman. His everything. Never had anything felt so right in his life.

Now he just needed her to catch up.

When she moved her hips, experimenting, and let out a soft gasp of excitement, he took that as a sign she was ready. Slowly, impossibly and achingly slowly, Kellen pulled himself out and entered her once more in a smooth motion. Over and over, he repeated the motion, keeping to a deliberate, measured pace as Raven learned what it was like to lay with a man.

And not just any man.

Her fated mate.

A man committed to giving her pleasure.

Love.

Protection.

He groaned, forcing his thoughts back, his body screaming for release.

"Is this...am I?"

"You're impossibly perfect, and I'm dying inside

because I want to release so badly, but I won't until you find your pleasure," Kellen groaned, continuing his slow, measured strokes.

"I, oh, but I've already...twice now." Raven gasped as he shifted the angle, lifting her hips slightly so he could drive deeper inside of her. "Kellen, that's...oh, yes, right there, right there, right there." And when she finally tipped over the edge, her muscles clenching around him, Kellen sought his own. A light flashed in the air around them, as he claimed her, crying out with his love for her.

His heart hammering in his chest, Kellen dropped to the mattress and pulled Raven into the crook of his arm so she sprawled half on top of him, and sighed in contentment.

"What was that flash of light? Did something happen?"

"I claimed you." Kellen yawned, both ready for sleep and for another exploration of Raven's body. She'd be tender, he reminded himself, this being her first time and all. "You're my fated mate."

"Kellen. I'm not..." Raven pushed back, sitting up, and Kellen sighed, knowing she was going to talk this to death. "You can't just claim me. That's positively barbaric. Don't I get a say in this?"

"Of course you do." Kellen yawned again, and realized he should probably prepare a bath for Raven. "I claimed you. But you still have to claim me."

"Well, I don't. I won't. That's just...you can't just..." Raven shook her head, her brow furrowed. "You don't just go around claiming people."

"Well no, not just anyone. But your fated mate you do.

And you, my love, are my fated mate. It's love for you that fills my very being, Raven."

"Love?" Raven arched an eyebrow at him. "Love? We hardly know each other. You can't love me."

"Nevertheless, my little nightbird, I do."

"You're...crazy. It's the battle. The magick. I don't know what. It's making you crazy, that's what it is."

"You just have to say you claim me back. Then we'll figure the rest out."

"What? I'm not doing that. I'm not claiming you. I'm *not*," Raven insisted when Kellen stood, unperturbed.

"That's fine. But I'd really prefer it if you would. Otherwise, I won't be with you all that long." Kellen held out a hand to Raven, and she glared at his hand and then up at him.

"Where are we going?"

"To have a bath together. You'll be tender, and I want to attend to you."

Raven's cheeks pinkened in that delightful manner she had when she was both embarrassed and intrigued about something. Relenting, she let him pull her from the bed.

"What do you mean you won't be around long if I don't claim you?"

"It's one of those Fae things you'll likely hate," Kellen said cheerfully, pleased to see the large tub was already full with steaming water. "If you don't claim me back, I'll eventually waste away and die."

"You'll what?" Raven screeched, rounding on him. "You absolute eejit. You can't just...no. No. I won't be responsible for your death. This is on you. You shouldn't have claimed me without my permission. You did this to yourself. I will not take responsibility for this. Absolutely not."

He wished he could tell her how adorable she looked, stomping her foot by the side of the bathtub, her hair mussed from their lovemaking, but he suspected it would infuriate her further.

"Okay," Kellen said, ever patient. Getting in the tub, he held out a hand to her. Raven eyed him suspiciously.

"What do you mean, okay? This feels like a trap."

"Get in the tub, Raven. We'll soak, get some sleep, and wake to fight the Dark Fae."

"And this whole fated mate thing? You'll just...let it go?"

"There's nothing to let go. You're my fated mate. I've claimed you. What you choose to do with that is on you."

When Raven lifted her chin at him, Kellen just grinned. He was too happy to worry much over unrequited claims. Naturally, Raven was nervous about this. They'd have time to sort it out.

"Come on in. The water's warm."

"No more talk of fated mates." Raven pointed a finger at him before she took his offered hand and settled into the tub. Reaching forward, Kellen dragged her onto his lap and just held her in silence, knowing there was nothing more he could say in this moment to convince her to take a chance on him.

"I love you, nightbird."

"Would you stop?" Raven hissed. But beneath the water, she squeezed his hand tightly, and Kellen grinned, before placing a kiss against her hair.

18

RAVEN

WHILE IT WAS a week of many firsts for her, waking up next to a man certainly topped the list. Raven snuggled backward, warmth blooming as Kellen's arm looped around her waist, pulling her close, and she gasped when his hands began to move. Slowly, he explored her body, lingering over areas that made her moan, whispering decadent thoughts at her neck, and when he entered her while spooning her, Raven's eyes almost crossed from the pleasure he brought her. By the time they made it from the room, breakfast was almost finished.

"Well, well, well. We wondered if we were going to have to send the guards in to drag you two out of there," Callum said, a smile hovering at his lips. Raven flushed, immediately embarrassed that everyone would know that they'd had sex. Seeming to understand her nerves, Kellen kept an arm around her shoulders.

"Raven's my fated mate," Kellen said, and Bianca squealed, clapping her hands together.

"I don't...we're not..." Raven glared up at Kellen, flustered.

"She's still coming to terms with it all. Let's give her space on that, shall we? In the meantime, have you reached a decision?"

"A decision on what?" Raven asked. She dropped into a chair and reached for a piece of bread, and a small pot of jam. She was famished. She knew what daily hunger was like, but this was something else entirely. *Apparently, a lot of sex tires a person out.* Although, Kellen certainly seemed full of energy.

"We were discussing if we would try the ritual first, before going to the Dark Realm," Bianca explained. "We've voted, but we'll wait to hear what you think."

"Oh, I can't possibly vote," Raven protested. "This isn't my place."

"You get a vote," Kellen said, placing a glass of juice by her plate and kissing the top of her head before taking the seat next to her. Raven was sure her cheeks were flaming. She'd never been comfortable with affection before, and the more Kellen touched her in public, the more it seemed to scream that they'd had sex. Was everyone looking at her differently? She certainly felt different. She picked up her glass and drank, before realizing that everyone was waiting for her to speak.

"Then I choose the path of less violence. If the ritual has the potential to take care of the Dark Goddess or whatever, wouldn't it make sense to give it a go first? It might save many lives." Raven looked down in shock at her now empty cup. She must have really been thirsty.

"See? I told you she'd agree with us." Bianca nodded her approval. "Kellen?"

"Ritual first," Kellen agreed.

"Where will we do it?" Seamus asked.

"In the square," Kellen said. "The people have a right to watch. It's their lives they are putting on the line."

"We'll just need..." Callum cocked his head as a guard appeared at the door.

"Sir. It's here."

"Perfect timing. Meet in the square in thirty minutes?" The king stood, and Lily followed him as he left, casting a quick smile back at the room.

"What was that about?" Raven asked.

"The amulets. Each Fae had to give up their ruling item to do the ritual. However, because it weakens the ruler to no longer have it, they've stayed behind to protect their people from a potential attack. Which is a shame, really, as I think you'd like some of the others." Bianca stood from the table. She looked well suited for battle today, with dark pants, a fitted coat, and heavy boots on her feet. "I need to retrieve Kellen's mother's ring from the magicks room, as well as the translation, and we should be ready to go."

"I have to admit, it's a lot to take in." Raven turned to Kellen. "Amulets. Rituals. Dark realms."

"Fated mates." Kellen grinned when Raven narrowed her eyes.

What was she going to do about him? Had the man completely lost his mind? They'd known each other less than a week, and he'd gone and pledged himself to her like...a maniac. An absolute maniac. And if she didn't claim him back then he was going to die? What kind of nonsense was that? Like she was supposed to know what she wanted for the rest of her life? Raven's whole life had been spent living day-to-day, and now Kellen was expecting her to just decide on her entire future. Her glare deepened as Kellen's grin widened.

"I don't like you very much right now," Raven said.

"I think you're lying. I think you like me more than you're willing to admit, and it scares you. But that's okay. I'm fine with giving you time."

"You don't have time though. You told me that last night. If I don't claim you back, you die." Just saying the words out loud infuriated her. She didn't want Kellen to die. She just didn't know if she wanted a future with him either. Raven was caught between a rock and a hard place and wasn't the least bit pleased about it. Whirling, she glared at Seamus who was doing his best to pretend he wasn't still in the room.

"Is that true? The whole fated mates thing? If I don't claim him back, or whatever, he'll die?" Raven asked.

"Yes, that's the way of it. Not immediately of course, it's kind of like a wasting disease. See, when fated mates claim each other, their magicks grow stronger. Incredibly so. But, everyone could just run around trying to claim each other as fated mates in order to get power, which is why the Fae long ago concocted the built-in safeguard. While many Fae do crave more power, they certainly don't at the expense of their lives."

"That makes zero sense," Raven argued. "If two

people fake claim each other, then they aren't really fated mates. So why would they get power?"

"Because sometimes a fated mate bond can grow after the fact."

"Then they would just deserve the power anyway, right? By your rules?"

"Not my rules." Seamus laughed. "But no, they wouldn't deserve the power if they entered into the pact for nefarious reasons."

"So he's just going to waste away unless I claim him. Can he take it back?" Raven asked.

"There's methods, yes," Seamus admitted, smiling when Kellen shook his head at him. "Sorry, man, I'm not going to lie to her."

"Take it back." Raven whirled on him. "I can't make this decision when I've only known you a week."

"It's not happening. You'll get used to the idea. Just think...you can actually be Queen Raven." With that, Kellen stood and crossed to where another guard had entered the room. After a quick conferral, he motioned to them both. "We're ready."

"Are we though? I feel like there's a lot more to discuss," Raven grumbled. But she stood, Seamus following her out, and they made their way to the square. Raven noticed what a drastic difference there was in the atmosphere this morning. Where last night had almost lent itself to a celebration of sorts, today they greeted with a sea of somber faces. Immediately, Raven lifted her head and began to scan the crowd, searching for anything amiss. Now wasn't the time to become complacent, she reminded herself. Just because she had a team to work with didn't mean she should stop looking out for her own safety.

A guard brought out a gold cauldron and set it on a table on the stage, and Raven's eyes almost bugged out of her head. If that thing was solid gold, she could only imagine the price it could fetch on the streets. Callum came out next, a gold circlet on his head, and for the first time she really saw him as the king when the entire crowd bowed respectfully. She'd forgotten for a while that he was king of all the Fae, instead thinking of him more like someone to pal around with a bit. She needed to be more careful there, because her mouth could often get her into trouble with those in positions of authority.

"Come with me," Kellen said at her ear, sliding an arm through hers. "I want to keep you close so I'm not worried about you while we're focusing on the ritual."

"I'm not sure I should be up there," Raven hissed, digging in her heels as he pulled her toward the platform where she'd sung from the depths of her soul the night before.

"Of course you should. You're my..." Kellen grinned when Raven rolled her eyes and elbowed him in the gut. They climbed the platform together, and though Raven tried to hang back, Kellen moved her firmly in front of him. For a guy that had been so hands off before, it seemed he took great joy in dragging her all over the place now. She *certainly* didn't plan on telling him that a very small part of her liked it when he manhandled her this way.

"Wait! Halt!" a voice shouted, before the ritual began. Confusion rippled through the crowd, and Raven tensed.

"Father?" Kellen asked, concern in his voice. Worry for his *father*, Raven noted, but not for himself. She didn't like this. Not one bit. Turning, she grabbed Kellen's elbow.

"Careful, Kellen. I don't trust him," Raven murmured, and Kellen glanced down at her.

"He's my father."

Raven pressed her lips together, stopping any other comments she wanted to make. She didn't come from a place of expertise when it came to the inner workings of familial relationships. If Kellen trusted his father, then she had to honor that.

"Devlin," King Callum nodded, acknowledging the man. "What seems to be the issue?"

"You'll need this to proceed with the ritual, won't you?" Devlin turned to the crowd, his voice crowing in delight, as he held up something that she couldn't see yet.

"What is it?" Raven hissed, and Bianca leaned close.

"I think it's their amulet."

"Oh. Oh," Raven breathed, realizing that it meant they could save Kellen's mother's ring instead of sacrificing it to the ritual.

"How did you get it?" Kellen demanded, his body rigid behind hers. "You told me the Domnua have it now."

"They did. We were breached again this morning. While you were curled up with your...with..." Devlin sneered at Raven, and she bared her teeth in response. God, but she hated little men with big egos.

"My fated mate?" Kellen supplied, his voice deadly.

"Is that right?" Devlin snorted out a laugh, and then

to everyone's surprise, he dismissed them by turning back to the crowd. "After a vicious battle, I've recovered the amulet. As I'm the holder of it now, I'm claiming my right to rule my people."

Kellen sucked in a breath behind her, and Raven froze, unsure of how to proceed. It seemed the crowd felt the same way, as many people glanced between Devlin and Kellen, uncertain of how to react.

"I said, I claim the right to the throne. Bow to me!" Devlin screamed, and to Raven's surprise a good portion of the crowd did. Seemingly appeased, Devlin nodded once before striding up to the platform.

"And you will bow to me," King Callum said, immediately asserting his authority, as he took the item that Devlin handed him. Though Raven strained to see what the amulet looked like, the king's hand concealed it. To Devlin's credit, he jerked his head in a quick bow, not foolhardy enough to ignore the king.

"Did you just steal the throne from me?" Kellen demanded, seeming to recover his speech.

"I don't think he has. Not really," Raven said, not caring if she broke some sort of weird Fae protocol. "Not even half your people acknowledged his demand. What kind of leader does that anyway? Walks in the door and demands immediate allegiance? Peacocking is what you're doing."

"And my first order of business will be to rule that all humans must leave the Fae realm." Devlin gave her a silky smile.

"Overruled," King Callum said, his tone mild. "Otherwise, you'd be telling me that you're ordering Lily to leave your castle, and I'm certain you're not doing that, are you?"

Devlin blanched. "No, sir."

"We'll sort this out later. For now, it's dangerous enough to have this many amulets in one place. We must proceed at once." The king held up his hand, calling for silence, and dug into the bag he held, as he read from the paper that Bianca held in front of him.

"By fire and water, earth and air"—King Callum pulled a necklace from the bag and dropped it into the cauldron, a puff of smoke rising into the air—"through night to day and dark to light..."

Something was wrong.

Raven didn't know what it was, she just *felt* it. Tuning out the king's words, she scanned the crowd, searching for whatever had put her on high alert. When nothing caught her eye, she turned back just as the king held the last amulet up.

It was the coin. The same coin she'd taken from Alistair's body the day he'd died. The coin that was currently resting in her pocket for safekeeping. It had never occurred to her that this was the Air Fae's missing amulet. In her mind, amulet had meant necklace or something statuesque, like a crown.

Which meant, whatever amulet that Devlin had handed off to the king was a fake, since Raven currently had the real one tucked away. Which *also* meant, if Kellen's mother's ring didn't go in the cauldron with the rest of the power items, the ritual wouldn't be complete.

"Wait!" Raven cried, lunging forward, but it was too late.

The coin had already dropped into the cauldron, the ritual now complete.

Devlin turned calculating eyes on her and threw his head back and laughed.

"Fools. All of you."

But the voice didn't come from Devlin. It came from over their heads, and when Devlin looked up and dropped to his knees, Raven's heart fell. She didn't want to look, didn't want to believe that Kellen's own father had just sold them out to the Dark Goddess. When her laughter split the sky, Raven's stomach twisted.

She should have claimed Kellen when she'd had the chance.

19

Kellen

Kellen's heart stilled.

His breath caught in his throat. His father, his own father, bowed in supplication to the Dark Goddess who rode the wind far above them.

The traitor came from his own blood.

His people gasped, screams ringing across the square, but there was nowhere to go. Nowhere to run. Domnua appeared from the shadows.

They were surrounded.

Unless he could lead his people through the tunnels, which was a dangerous endeavor with so many of them in such a small space, and only a few paths ending in exit points. Plus, who was to say that Domnu didn't have those exits covered? If she'd been working with his father, then she'd likely know every entry point to the castle. Fury roiled in his stomach, along with a bone-deep sadness. The man he'd thought was just grieving had been revealed as a bloody traitor. Betraying his own son, forsaking his own people, leading them all into darkness. *What the hell?*

"Father...how could you? What were you thinking?" Kellen demanded, pulling Raven tight to his side as Domnu drifted slowly to the ground, his people drawing back, pressing themselves against the walls in a bid to get away from the Dark Goddess.

"I was thinking how weak you were." Devlin laughed. "And how our people needed a steady hand. The guidance of our one true ruler." He bowed his head as Domnu approached, a smile hovering on her face.

She was starkly, horrifically beautiful, all sharp angles and icy eyes. Her dark hair writhed around her head, a nest of snakes that snapped at the people she passed, and she wore a dark gown of leather and lace.

"It doesn't have to be so hard, does it now?" Domnu all but purred, arching an eyebrow at Kellen. "Swear to me your allegiance, and your people will be saved."

"Never," Kellen said, gritting his teeth. "My father may betray his son, but I will never betray my people."

"Families are...difficult, aren't they?" Domnu tapped a finger against her lips as she prowled among his people, smiling as they shrunk back from the snakes that hissed at them. "Take my darling sister. She's been nothing but a thorn in my side for centuries now. I suppose celebrating the holidays has been a touch lonely without her, but we do the best we can when we lose people we care about, don't we?"

"You care about her? About Goddess Danu?" Kellen's eyes widened at Bianca's question before he remembered that this wasn't her first time facing off with the Dark Goddess. "Why do I find that so hard to believe?"

"Speaking of thorns in my side..." Domnu grimaced as her eyes landed on Bianca. "You again. You do seem to be quite resilient, don't you? Even for a human. I suspect you'll make an excellent addition to my army."

"Not likely. I'm horrible at taking orders." Bianca grinned cheerfully, and to Kellen's surprise, Domnu laughed. It wasn't a cheerful sound. No, it was more like babies screaming in the night, and it sent a shiver down his spine.

"Noted." Domnu strolled forward until she stood directly in front of the group who stood on the platform, and Kellen was certain she was going to address the king. Except her eyes weren't on Callum.

She'd stopped in front of Raven.

The expression on her face shifted, morphing from one of abject evil to warmth. Well, as warm as a Dark Goddess of the underworld could be. Even the snakes that coiled around her head calmed, ceasing their hissing noises, and turned to blink curious eyes at Raven.

Kellen didn't know what was about to happen, but he didn't like where this was going. Shoving Raven behind him, he stepped forward, but before he could do anything, Domnu spoke.

"As I mentioned, family can be complicated. Nevertheless, we're all connected by our blood, aren't we? And in the end, it's the blood that binds, isn't it? The time has come, daughter, for you to join me as we step into power, together."

A roaring sounded in Kellen's ears, heat racing down

the back of his neck, as he turned in what felt like slow motion at Raven's gasp.

"No," Kellen breathed. It was too much. First Alistair, then his father, and now...now his fated mate had betrayed him as well? Rage flashed through him, like a hot knife slicing through butter, and Callum grabbed his arms before he swung at the goddess. She laughed, delighted at his anger, and lifted her chin at him.

"There you go, you silly little Fae. *Feed* the anger. Let it fuel your blood. It's what I thrive on the most. In anger lies power." Domnu smirked before turning back to face Raven.

Her daughter.

Now, as Kellen struggled for breath, and Callum and Seamus held him back, he watched the two women study each other. His heart sank. Seeing them like this, in silhouette, he could see it. *He could see it.*

Mother and daughter.

Of the same blood.

It sickened him, that he'd claimed her, that he'd let her into his bed. All this time she'd played him, just like his father had, and now the Fae would die because of their evil.

"Daughter. You're looking well." Domnu looked Raven up and down and sniffed. "Though your wardrobe could use an upgrade."

Raven's mouth worked, but nothing came out, and her hand went to a necklace at her throat that Kellen hadn't noticed her wearing before.

"*You*?" Raven finally spoke, her face inscrutable. She stood, frozen.

"Yes, my dearest one. I've come for you. Can't you feel it? When I'm close? The call to power thrums in your blood. You've always been destined for this, my child. The time has come. You're needed to help rule. Together we'll fly."

"All these years..." Raven whispered, and Domnu waved her words away, turning to where Kellen snarled at her.

"Your fated mate carries secrets from you. Do you know that? She's had the amulet all along. Now that the others have been destroyed, she's the strongest of all the Fae."

"No." Bianca stepped forward, shaking her head. "No, Raven. That can't be true."

"But it is. Isn't it, my dear?" When Raven said nothing, her expression like stone, Domnu strode forward and reached a hand into Raven's jacket pocket. Raven remained frozen, whether through fear or Domnu's magick, and when Domnu turned, the amulet in her hand, his heart shattered.

A collective gasp went through the crowd, and Domnu laughed, enjoying the drama of it all, before tucking the coin back in Raven's pocket. Gently she ran a hand over Raven's brow, a look of love hovering on her evil face.

"My beautiful daughter. It's time. Join me in the Dark Realm, and we'll be unstoppable. Together, our power will grow wider, and the world will never be the same."

"Don't go, Raven," Bianca ordered, trying to capture Raven's attention. "*We* love you, Raven. She doesn't. It doesn't matter if she's your mother. We'll love you anyway. Don't leave with her. You don't have to do this."

"Oh, but I think she wants to." Domnu beamed as Raven stepped forward, her face still betraying no emotion. Had she completely shut down? Kellen couldn't understand what she was doing. Where had the tough, feisty woman he'd known gone? Instead, she looked numbed, like she wasn't even really there. Raven didn't spare Kellen a single glance, only keeping her eyes trained on Domnu.

Her mother.

"I'll go." Raven's words were but a whisper, yet they carried the impact of a sledgehammer.

"Brilliant." Domnu reached out and grabbed Raven's arm, and before any of them could react, the two disappeared from sight. Kellen dropped to his knees, his head in his hands, as his world crumbled. It didn't matter now, what would happen, for he had a death sentence hanging over his head. Raven had never claimed him back, and now that she was gone, he couldn't revoke his claim. His love, his fated mate, was a daughter of the Dark Goddess, and together, they were going to destroy the world as he knew it.

Laughter danced across the air, and the rage that Kellen had barely kept contained unleashed. He was on top of his father before the others could stop him. Slamming his fist into Devlin's face, Kellen was rewarded with a satisfying crunching sound and blood sprayed from his father's nose. The man crumpled, but still Kellen didn't stop, delivering punishing blows until Callum finally pulled him off.

"You'll kill him. Stop it. This is an order from your king." Callum's voice was sharp at his ear, and the haze that covered Kellen's eyes faded. Looking down at where his father now lay in a bloody pulp on the ground, Kellen spat on him.

"That's enough." Callum drew him away. Kellen's fists stung, but he welcomed the pain. He wanted more of it, actually, *anything* other than to think about how Raven had just left with the Dark Goddess.

"Don't believe it." Kellen looked up at where Lily stood, wringing her hands, sympathy on her face. "Don't let Domnu trick you. I don't know what's going on, but Raven wouldn't betray you."

"She wouldn't," Bianca agreed, stepping forward with a towel to wipe Kellen's hands.

"She just did," Kellen bit out. He wanted to scream at them all to shut up, to stop talking, to just leave him alone, but even Kellen couldn't bring himself to yell at sweet Lily.

"She may have her own reasons. She's never known a mother. Maybe she just needed to get some questions answered," Lily offered.

"While betraying every last one of us in the process."

"I'll admit, it does look bad," Bianca said, but she shook her head, confusion in her eyes. "But it doesn't ring true. Something's not landing for me."

"Lovely. Let me know when you figure out what it is. In the meantime, I'll be drinking myself into a stupor."

Kellen strode away, not addressing his people, no longer caring what happened. Why should he? His world had been shattered.

Something glinted on the ground at his feet, and he picked it up, realizing it was the necklace that Raven had worn. Turning it over, he read the ancient Fae inscription, and his stomach dropped. Closing his eyes, he brought the necklace to his heart.

Bloodsong.

Only those of the same blood can kill a goddess.

Only those of the same blood...

Was she ... No, surely not.

Was Bianca right?

Was Raven not betraying them at all?

Was she sacrificing herself?

That bloody idiot. Kellen whirled.

"I take that back. Let's go get our girl."

"What changed your mind?" King Callum asked, glancing down at the necklace that Kellen held.

"You're all right. If Raven is the woman I think, well, I hope she is...then she's not jumping ship to side with her mother. Sure, it's probably a shock to learn who her mother is, particularly like this, but Raven's not dumb, and she's quick to think on her feet. She's a survivor and has been that way for a really long time. We're the first people she's had...that really cared about her."

"She's protecting us," Lily said, her face wreathed in concern.

"Is she buying us time? Leading Domnu away from here?" Seamus asked.

"I think it's worse. Much worse than that." Kellen grimaced.

"Oh, no." Bianca reached out and gripped Kellen's

arm. "She's not. She wouldn't. Not without us there to help. That's too much to take on…"

"What's happening?" Callum demanded.

"She's going to try and kill Domnu. Even if it means she dies trying," Bianca said, fear in her eyes.

"We ride now," Kellen ordered. The clock was ticking, and he had no idea how long Raven would be able to keep up her ruse with Domnu.

Bianca cheered, and even Callum smiled at his words.

"You're certain?"

"Yes, but someone needs to lock him up," Kellen pointed to his unconscious father.

"I doubt he's going anywhere anytime soon." Nevertheless, Callum snapped his fingers and the guards carried Devlin away.

Straightening, Kellen raised his hands in the air and stepped into the leadership role that he'd been meant for all along.

"My people, gather close. The time has come to take back what is ours."

20

RAVEN

A STICKY NAUSEA swam through Raven's stomach as she rocked backward on her heels, taking in her surroundings. The magickal trip from the castle in the sky to the Dark Realm had been dizzying and disconcerting, like the particles of her body were being rearranged and put back together again. Raven took a moment to steady herself. Though she didn't move, her eyes darted around, taking in as much of her surroundings as she could.

The sky was different here. A hazy green color, like a polluted city river, showcasing murky yellow clouds. The landscape was bare, like a barren winter's day, as though not a single flower dared to try and bloom here. And it was still.

No breeze.

No birdsong.

No sounds of laughter. *No dancing, happy Alicorns.*

Raven had read once that a forest will go quiet when a

predator arrived, and now she was reminded of that as Domnu turned, her arms held wide, eyes alight with delight.

"Welcome home, my dearest girl. I've hated having to bide my time, to wait to show you what I could give to you, but the time was never right. Now, *now*, it is. We'll rule together, as it was always destined to be."

"Two goddesses?" Raven forced herself to look, really look, at this abomination that was her mother. Bile rose in her throat. "Isn't that your sister and you, then? I'm not a goddess that I'm aware of."

"Danu can hardly call herself a goddess," Domnu muttered, and the snakes around her head chattered in agreement. "She's weak, and a fool. She had a chance for power and squandered it. But that's neither here nor there, Raven. We're together now, and together, you and I are unstoppable."

Raven's stomach churned, and she tried to force herself to affect nonchalance, while her thoughts whirled in her head. Would Kellen know that she hadn't meant to betray him? Everything had happened so fast that Raven had been momentarily stunned. When her thoughts finally caught up with her shock, she'd quickly realized she'd have to make a decision fast before the scene dissolved into chaos. And so she'd gone. Breaking his heart in the process, Raven was sure of it, but someday, yes someday, hopefully he'd forgive her.

She had to go.

That was, quite simply, the only choice.

Not only was she now the only one that could kill Domnu, but she also was the only one who was expendable. Kellen's people needed him. And the others? They were all contributing to bettering society for everyone. But Raven? What did she really matter? Sure, she put a smile on people's faces once in a while with a merry tune on the side of the road. But at the end of the day, she'd lived on the fringe her whole life. Nobody to miss her when she was gone.

But now?

If she had to go, then she was going to go out in a momentous way. One that changed the course of history forever on. It was worth it, if it meant that Bianca would keep smiling, and Lily would keep dreaming, and Kellen...her heart shuddered at the thought of him.

He'd be okay. He had the others. And Riker. Riker would be there for him, flying him to the waterfall to rejuvenate. Kellen would find someone more suitable to love, and life would move on.

And she would ensure that it would, by her own sacrifice.

"What's wrong?" Domnu narrowed her eyes at Raven, and the snakes inched forward, mirroring her look. "I thought you would be happy about becoming one of the most powerful women in all of history."

Going with her instincts, Raven decided to lean on truth more than trying to lie and pretend she was happy to be here. If Domnu was smart at all, and she likely had to be based on how many people she'd convinced to be on her side through the years, then she'd see through Raven's act anyway.

"It's not about that." Raven crossed her arms over her chest and channeled the angst of an angry teenager.

She'd had plenty of experience with it, what with volunteering at the youth group, and now she tossed her hair over her shoulder and glared at Domnu. The goddess raised an eyebrow in surprise. "If you want to know, not that you even give a shit, but I'm mad at you."

"You're...what? What did you say?" Domnu's mouth dropped open in surprise. "You're angry? With me? When I'm offering you unimaginable power?"

"Yes, *Mother*." The word sliced like razor blades against her tongue. "I'm mad, furious, actually with you."

"I can't say that I understand." Domnu's face darkened, and Raven hastened to explain before she fell from the tightrope she was walking.

"You see, Mother, you left me. My whole life...I've been alone. Everybody else...they had mothers. Mothers to hold them when they cried. Mothers to tell secrets to. Mothers who brought them soup when they were sick. Mothers who ensured their daughters had a home to live in...so they weren't forced to live on the streets with no food or money or shelter." To Raven's great surprise, her voice cracked, but she continued. "But where were you? I was all alone."

"But Raven...I couldn't keep you with me," Domnu said, drifting closer, her face now a mask of concern. "I was in exile after the Four Treasures curse broke. It wasn't safe for you to be with me, yet I knew one day I'd bring you back to rule by my side."

"I was all alone!" Raven shouted, letting the anger come. Because she *was* angry. For years, she'd been forced to fight for her safety, her food, daily, and for the most part, she was so used to it that it didn't bother her.

But it had never been her choice. Those choices had all been taken from her. Because this monster before her had left her. "*You* left *me*. You left. I had nobody. I had to figure it all out on my own. I was just a child. Just a child." She punctuated the words with her finger, fury making her vibrate. It wasn't that she wanted Domnu for a mother—nobody in their right mind would want that kind of evil in their lives—but she drew on every drop of insecurity she'd ever felt about being abandoned and blasted Domnu with it. "I hate you. I hate you for leaving me. I hate you for not caring that all those nights I sat in the cold, damp, darkness...shivering on the side of the street, certain that I would die in the night, that you just...you never came. You never came for me. You just didn't care. You only care about yourself, it seems."

"I've heard of this," Domnu said, tapping her finger on her lips as she paced in front of Raven. "I've heard of daughters getting angry with their mothers. This is what it feels like, isn't it? Is this...am I feeling regret? What is this feeling?"

To Raven's shock, the Dark Goddess held her hand to her stomach and turned to Raven with confusion.

"Are you asking me what emotions feel like?" Raven asked. An idea occurred to her, as it seemed that the dynamic was shifting, and maybe she should play this to her advantage.

"I believe that I might be. I don't think I like it." Domnu screwed up her face as she thought about it, and Raven realized that she needed to keep the goddess in this space of confusion, instead of calculating the downfall of the good Fae.

"Well, do something about it then. You can make it up to me." It killed Raven to say that, but if she could give Domnu another task, one that she considered worthwhile, it might distract her long enough. What she wanted was an apology, from mother to daughter, for abandoning her all these years. And...yet, when she stood here and looked at this monster, Raven realized it didn't really matter. She'd never look at this woman and see a mother, let alone *her* mother, and there would be no redemptive arc for their relationship. An apology would do nothing but make Raven angry, because then she'd have to actually accept that Domnu was fallible, and frankly, as an immortal Dark Goddess, she really had no excuse to be.

"Make it up to you?" Domnu whirled in a circle, clutching her arms around her chest, clearly someone who had a flair for dramatics. "You want me to make things better with you. What an interesting concept. I don't think I've ever done something like that before. What would that entail?"

"I honestly don't know." Raven couldn't tell who was more startled, her or Domnu, when she laughed. This situation had reached an absurdity level that required laughter or tears, and Raven was not going to waste her tears for this woman. "You can't just show up, tell me you're my mother, and expect me to, *like*, love you. We don't even know each other. You're talking about ruling kingdoms together, and I didn't even know I had magick. It's a huge learning curve."

"I think I'm beginning to understand this. You're absolutely right...and this will be quite fun, won't it?"

Domnu clapped her hands together like a delighted child. "I'll teach you everything about my kingdom and our dark magick. Of course, my love, this makes perfect sense. That was foolish of me to think that you'd be able to just step into the role of ruler. Even though it is in your blood, not everyone is suited to being a ruler." Domnu sniffed. "Like my embarrassment of a sister."

"I wouldn't know." Raven shrugged. "I only learned about the Fae a week ago. I don't know about your sister, well, my aunt, and I guess about anything much else. Or my father even."

"Your father." Domnu stilled, and her eyes flashed. A chill rippled across Raven's skin, and she worried that she might have pushed it too far.

"I'm guessing he was a jerk?" Raven decided to play the sympathetic card. It was clear that Domnu was more childlike than motherly, used to her every whim being indulged.

"The worst," Domnu said, shaking her head in disgust while her snakes did the same.

"Men, ugh," Raven said, making a sound of disgust.

"Really, quite worthless, the whole lot of them. However, I needed his seed and what was done is done. I got rid of him afterwards. There was no point in keeping him around once I'd conceived."

Raven froze. The casual manner in which Domnu spoke of murdering her lover, Raven's father, reminded Raven exactly who she was dealing with. Though her mother was being friendly with her now, it was a grave reminder that the woman could turn on her at any second. At the same time, weren't those Raven's intentions?

Like mother, like daughter.

It hurt, more than it should have, to know that the apple didn't fall far from the tree. In the end, even if she fought on the side of the light, she'd still have blood on her hands. Though her chances of survival were slim at best, she'd known that when she'd agreed to come here.

"He was...human?" Raven asked, starting forward when Domnu gestured for her to walk alongside her.

"Not fully, no. Of the songbird tribe."

"I'm sorry, what? What is that?" Was her mother saying she was descended from a bird?

"Hmm, they're both gods and animals. They shift between the two forms. There are various tribes of them. The songbirds are the least annoying, in my opinion, and he did quite amuse me with his music."

"He sang to you?" Raven's heart clenched. He actually didn't sound all that bad. Maybe that's where she got her love of music from. Maybe, if Domnu hadn't killed him, she would have led a very different life.

"Nonsense really. His magick wasn't powerful enough for mine, but I suppose he was amusing for a moment. Until he wasn't."

"What happened?" Raven wanted to know what had caused the Dark Goddess to turn on a man willing to make love to her and sing her silly songs.

"He wanted forever." Domnu shrugged. "Nobody had wanted that before with me, which meant it was likely in a bid for my power. So, he had to go."

And this was why he was a jerk? The man had put up

with Domnu and then pledged love to her and she'd killed him for it?

"Enough about him," Domnu snapped. Crossing the barren field, she paused. "It's time to complete our journey."

"Where are we going?" Raven asked, needing to shift the conversation away from speaking of her father for fear she might say something to cause Domnu to turn on her.

"My castle. It's much nicer than that embarrassingly pitiful one you were just at. Now you'll see what power really looks like." Domnu paused and waved a hand in the air. The barren landscape in front of them shimmered and shifted, like when someone throws a pebble in the smooth surface of a pond, and suddenly an entire city materialized before them. Raven's mouth dropped open, and a shiver drifted over her skin. The whole time they'd been talking, Raven had thought it was just the two of them. But once Domnu lifted the illusion, she saw that she was surrounded by hundreds of those same silvery Fae that she'd killed.

Wait, she *had* killed already. Even if the Domnua were different from the Fae she'd met and befriended, had they still deserved to die at her hand? Kill or be killed. Was that the way of it in the Dark Realm? Raven took a deep breath to steady herself as the army parted for Domnu and she marched up to the most imposing building that Raven had ever seen. Made of obsidian glass and all sharp corners and spiky edges, it reminded her of an executioner's wet dream. Not a soft or comforting corner in sight, instead the castle gleamed with malice.

"Gorgeous," Raven murmured. If you were someone that enjoyed casual torture for a living, that is.

"Isn't it?" Domnu cooed, trailing a finger along a gold sconce shaped in the form of a skull with bleeding eye sockets. "Shall we dine? Have a glass of wine? Is that what mothers and daughters do together?"

"It's a starting point," Raven agreed. Her stomach felt like someone was hacking at it with a knife, and she worried that perhaps her plan had been overly optimistic. At the time, when they were standing alone in a barren field, she'd been more confident about taking down the Dark Goddess. But now, surrounded by an army of Domnua in a castle that looked like every piece of décor could be a weapon, Raven wasn't feeling so sure of her decision.

You're not going to get out of this alive.

The thought almost brought tears to her eyes, and she had to will them back as she followed her mother into a large dining room. There was no use crying about the reality of the path she'd chosen. The sooner she accepted her fate, the quicker she'd be able to make her move.

What did it matter then, if she ate a fancy dinner with her mother and indulged in a glass of wine? Raven now understood, she could feel it in her bones, that she wouldn't see the light of dawn again.

In a matter of moments, servants had appeared and spread the table with food, and Raven was ushered into a seat. Domnu looked the table over with an eagle eye, and then gave a sharp nod, dismissing the help.

"This looks nice, doesn't it?" Domnu looked strangely uncertain as she turned to Raven. "I...frankly I always dine alone. I don't put much thought to the needs of others. Will this suit you, daughter?"

"It suits," Raven quickly agreed. "Truly, there's more food here than I could ever eat. Thank you for bringing it."

"Go on then. Enjoy." Domnu waved a hand. Though Raven wasn't certain she could actually break bread with her mother, she did pick up her glass of wine. Waiting until Domnu did as well, she tapped her glass to her mother's. A pleased smile hovered on Domnu's lips, and the snakes slithered around her head, smiling as well. The hair was such an odd thing, like a mirror of her mood, and Raven desperately wanted to ask about it. Instead, she waited until Domnu took the first sip, having watched a servant pour them wine from the same jug, and then she took a sip as well.

The wine was delicious.

At least she couldn't fault her mother's taste.

The amulet thrummed in her pocket, a gentle reminder that she was stronger for carrying it, and Raven hoped it would give her the edge she needed to do what she had to do.

"I don't know how to start getting to know you," Raven surprised Domnu by saying, and paused when her mother looked at her in annoyance. Domnu then seemed to realize she was supposed to be carrying on a conversation with her daughter and waved at her to go ahead. "I'm just going to ask the first question that pops in my head. Is that okay?"

"Was that the question?" Domnu arched an eyebrow.

"No." Raven smiled. "The first question that popped in my head is...what is your greatest wish? Or I guess... what do you want the most?"

"That's an odd question. Why do you ask that?"

Because if you know what people want the most, then you know how to hurt them.

"I think that's how people bond. By sharing the things they like, what they dream about, that kind of thing." Could this conversation be any more awkward? Raven took another sip of her wine and reached over to spoon some food on her plate. She still didn't plan to eat but didn't want to be rude. *Oh the irony. Not wanting to be rude before an evil goddess.*

"What do I want most?" Domnu laughed. "It's simple, really. I want the world to know my name. I want every last human, Fae, and otherworldly being to answer to me and know that my word is law."

"So, just a little bit of world domination," Raven mused. "No tall order there."

"It is a tall order," Domnu said, giving her a look, and Raven realized that nobody likely ever teased the Dark Goddess.

"I was teasing," Raven explained. "I understand what you want is a big deal. It was just a little joke."

"You're *teasing* me?"

"Yes?" Raven pressed her lips together and hoped she hadn't made a mistake.

"How unusual. I'm not sure I like it. I think that I do though."

"Did you want me to try again?"

"Another tease?" Domnu leveled a look at her. "I'm not certain. I've likely had enough."

Tough crowd.

"By all means, I'll be on my best behavior then."

"And what is it you want most then, daughter?" Domnu tilted her head at Raven.

Love.

It was Raven's first thought, something that had always hovered in the backdrop of her life, this seemingly unattainable thing that the rest of the world was so easily afforded. But she couldn't say that to a woman who didn't even understand what a joke was and killed her lover after sex.

"A family," Raven finally said and Domnu beamed.

"A small wish. And something I can easily give you. Not only do you have me now, but you have all of them." Domnu nodded to where hundreds of Domnua wandered below them in the square. "Albeit, they are a bit dumb. But useful, nonetheless. And that's all that matters, right?"

The sentiment summed up exactly what a Dark Goddess would view people as—tools. And they fell into two categories. Useful or expendable. No, Domnu could never really give her family, and that, in its own weird way, was her biggest gift to Raven.

21

KELLEN

BEFORE THE FIRST light of dawn, the Air Fae rode, having agreed to meet at the Earth Fae's realm. Terra, leader of the Earth Fae, had the most intricate network of portals to work with, and the Elemental armies would join forces to enter the Dark Realm at the same time.

They'd each go through separate portals, accessing the realm from every entrance they could find, with the hopes to wipe out Domnu's army and, if they couldn't kill her, at the very least render her powerless for centuries to come.

Kellen only wanted Raven back.

As soon as Riker landed on a grassy knoll cocooned by a dense stand of trees, he jumped to the ground and stalked toward where Terra stood.

"Is everything in place? We must move at once."

He'd met the Earth Fae leader a few times over the years, and she was known to be a well-respected ruler.

She wore a green tunic with a gold breast plate, a sword at her side.

"Welcome, Kellen. It's good to see you again," Terra said, lifting her chin to look up at him. Kellen winced as she graciously ignored his rudeness.

"Apologies. We're..."

"His fated mate is about to sacrifice herself by trying to kill Domnu on her own," Bianca said from behind him, and Terra's eyes widened.

"Your impatience is understood, and your rudeness forgiven." Reaching out, Terra squeezed his arm. "The leaders are here. Our magick will be more powerful if we do a ritual before we leave. If your fated mate is there alone, we can send her support."

"We can?" Kellen asked, surprised.

"Of course." Terra smiled and tapped a bare foot to the grass. "The Earth knows. We'll speak to her."

"Anything we can do to help. I'm...I'm scared it might be too late." Bianca gripped Kellen's arm, leaning into him in a show of support, and he allowed it. If his mother couldn't be here with him, Bianca seemed an excellent stand-in.

"Come." Terra beckoned them toward a circle of standing stones where a group of men and women stood.

"Imogen and Nolan, speaking for the sea." Imogen and Nolan stepped forward, greeting everyone, before moving to one side of the circle.

"Sorcha and Torin, who fight fire with fire." Another couple walked forward, each of them all but vibrating with energy, and took their place.

"Terra and Rian." Terra smiled at the man who must

be her fated mate and walked with him to her side of the circle. "We stand for Mother Earth."

"And Kellen." Kellen spoke for himself as he took up the last spot in the circle. He didn't miss that he was standing on his own, but there was nothing to be done about it. "Flying for the Air Fae."

Were Raven with him...she would be at his side. The night before had been unbearable, knowing she was gone. That he'd lost her even though he'd only just met her. How was it possible to fall so completely in love with someone in such a short time? *We have to get her back.*

"King Callum and Lily," Terra called, pointing to the middle of the circle. "You fight for all." The two went to stand in the middle.

"Whoops, I think we need to just jump out of the circle." Bianca moved to grab Seamus's arm.

"No, Bianca. You join us in the middle. The both of you have fought as selflessly as if you ruled a throne yourselves. You deserve to stand at the side of a king," Lily spoke up, her voice soft, but sure.

"She's right." King Callum smiled down at his love. "Join us, please. It's an honor to have you at our sides."

"Oh well, now you've gone and done it." Bianca fanned her face, where tears shone in her eyes. Together the two hurried to stand in the middle of the circle. They all looked expectantly at Terra, who seemed to know the ritual she had in mind.

"What is your fated mate's name?" Terra asked Kellen.

"Raven," Kellen said. Her name rasped at his throat, spearing his heart, and he hoped, desperately, that she still lived.

"Raven. Bird of the night. I wonder..." Terra tapped her fingers and then turned to the forest, a complicated whistle of a song leaving her lips. A whisper of wind carried it to the trees, their leaves reaching out to collect the message and carry it along. Silence descended, and Kellen waited, his impatience growing as every crucial second passed. Just as he was about to speak, Terra looked to the sky, her eyes brightening.

A shadow loomed.

"Just as I thought. Your mate is a powerful one, Kellen." Terra beamed, and Kellen's eyes widened as the sky descended into darkness. Not from storm clouds, oh no, but from hundreds of thousands of ravens that flew on the wind, in perfect synchronicity, ready to join the fight.

"That's so cool," Bianca breathed.

"Our purpose with this ritual is twofold," Terra intoned, and Kellen focused on her words, as the birds swooped in perfect circles over their heads. "We seek to send power to Raven, who fights alone in the Dark Realm, and to give protection to ourselves and our people as we embark on the greatest battle of our lifetime."

The severity of what they were about to do slammed home, and Kellen almost staggered under the weight of it all. He'd already lost almost everything. Would he be strong enough to do this? An image of Raven, laughing over a chubby baby Alicorn flashed into his mind. And then another image of her, as just a child, huddled under a dark bridge, crying herself to sleep at night.

Nobody had ever fought for her before. Raven deserved a chance. A chance at love, a chance at life, a chance to show the world what she was made of. Her songs deserved to see the light.

"As water feeds the earth,
and air breathes life to fire,
We unite with all our worth,
For we shall never tire,
To the Dark Realm we go,
With power on our side,
Fate may play her hand
But true love will abide.
When she sings,
queens will fall,
daughters of blood,
end them all."

Light flashed, the circle of stones momentarily catching fire, and the earth rumbled beneath them as magick poured like a river of molten gold into the crust of the earth's core, and then winked from sight. Smiling, Terra released her hands and stepped forward.

"It is done. We go now, to help our sister in the Dark Realm. Imogen and Nolan will go by sea, Sorcha and Torin through the fire portals, we'll go through the caves, and you, Kellen..."

"The sky portal." Kellen looked up to where the ravens hovered. "They'll come with me?"

"That's the plan. If you fly first, they will follow."

"We'll go with you, Kellen." Seamus came forward and clapped his arm around Kellen's shoulders. Warmth slipped through him. He hadn't realized just how much he needed the support.

"While I'm certainly not saying that I have a favorite

Elemental..." Bianca looked around at the others apologetically, "but, he does have Alicorns sooo..."

"I don't blame you." Sorcha, a petite woman with flaming red hair laughed. "You owe us a ride when this is over, Kellen."

"When this is over, we'll have a huge celebration, and everyone can enjoy the Alicorns. If they allow it, of course."

The ravens began to caw above them, and a shiver danced over Kellen's skin.

"The time is now." Terra grabbed Rian's hand and pulled him toward a path. In moments, everyone had disappeared to their portals.

"We'll fly with you as well, Kellen. It will give us a good view of what is going on below us," King Callum said, motioning to where their Alicorns waited. Behind them, hundreds of Air Fae mounted their own Alicorns and took to the sky.

Kellen leapt onto Riker's back and was already in the air before he was fully seated. His breath caught as they rose, a prayer at his lips.

The Alicorns flew, the stark white of their wings contrasting with the blanket of black ravens, looking like hundreds of lily petals strewn across the surface of dark water. Dark to light.

United.

They approached the portal, a barely discernable shiver of a cloud in the sky, and Kellen took the lead.

"Riker, through the portal." Kellen leaned close to the Alicorn's ear. "At any point, if you need to lead your family back, then do so. Do not, and I mean this with every ounce of my being, do not sacrifice them for me. I can fight on my own two feet. Promise me."

Friend.

"Yes, friend. But family also. Understood?"

The waterfall image projected into his mind and Kellen smiled. When all of this was over, he'd take Riker and Raven there and they would play in the cool waters of the stream, knowing that the world was once again safe from darkness.

They passed through the portal, the air shifting around them, the atmosphere growing thick and murky as they entered the Dark Realm. They flew in silence, over a scrappy barren landscape, and Kellen shifted, turning to look at Callum.

Callum shook his head, as though to indicate that something wasn't right, and Kellen turned forward just in time to catch a small ripple in the illusion. He pointed, not daring to speak, and Callum caught what he was showing him. The king held his hands up, muttering words under his breath, and the illusion dissolved.

Alarms sounded as the *true* Dark Realm was revealed.

Instantly, they were thrown into battle. Even Kellen, who had the advantage of being on the offensive, was surprised by the onslaught. Below them a gleaming black castle with spiky turrets dominated a city where thousands of Domnua poured forth from their hidey-holes, like someone had kicked an ants' nest. The city met the ocean, the water a greasy golden-brown color like spilled oil, and in it, the Water Fae surfaced, tridents in hand. Fire exploded in a rushing wave across the hills, like lava pouring down the slopes of a volcano, as Sorcha and

Torin arrived. The earth rumbled, shifting, as Terra joined Sorcha and they marched on foot toward the castle, warriors with a mission, their men at their sides.

"Ahead!" Bianca cried and Kellen looked up to see a flock of...dragons? No, it wasn't dragons flying their way. They were reptilian, almost raptor like, like an eagle that had been plucked of all its feathers and flew on shiny wings of skin. Domnua clung to their backs, weapons raised, and the ravens met them full force.

Riker pushed forward, spearing a Domnua with a bolt of fire from his horn, as the ravens overwhelmed the raptors, pecking at their eyes, their wings, ripping bits of flesh and skin apart until one by one the prehistoric birds dropped from the sky, their riders tumbling from their backs.

A flash of lavender caught his eye and Kellen turned Riker away.

Far below, Domnu raced across an outside wall of the castle, Raven at her side, and ducked into another wing of the castle. Relief swept through him.

She still lived.

Which meant they stood a fighting chance. The songs of his people, and those who went before him, filled his blood and he turned, raising an arm into the air.

"Dance on the wind. We side, we side, with the light," Kellen sang with all his heart, as the Air army pivoted as one and dove toward the castle.

"Dance on the wind...for today, *today*, we fight," Kellen whispered, hope filling his heart.

22

RAVEN

"HOW DARE THEY?" Domnu seethed, snapping her fingers so the door slammed behind her and Raven. At the first shout of warning, Domnu had been on her feet, dragging Raven through the castle, across the parapet, and into a weapons room.

For a brief moment, when they had been outside, Raven had glanced to the sky.

Fear gripped her, clawing at her throat, as she saw the Alicorns suspended in the air, thousands of ravens surrounding them, and otherworldly dinosaur-like demon raptors on the attack.

Kellen.

He was here. The Alicorns were here. No, no, no. Raven could've kicked herself. She should have made her move sooner. Now the people she cared about were going to get hurt.

"Do they honestly think they stand a chance against

my power? They are nothing. *Nothing*. A speck of dust to be wiped off my lapel," Domnu seethed as she snapped her fingers once more and her gown changed to a shiny patent leather bodysuit that matched her castle décor nicely. Slipping a silver shield embedded with onyx from the wall, she strapped it to her front like a chest plate. "Take one."

Raven's eyes widened as she realized that Domnu expected her to go into battle at her side. Of course she did. She truly thought they were in this together, that the two of them would take over the world. On one hand, this worked in Raven's favor, on the other, it would look horrible to her friends when she stepped outside by Domnu's side. Knowing she had little choice, as the game was already in motion, Raven stepped forward and picked a chest plate, looping the straps over her shoulders and tying them at her back.

"What weapon do you prefer?" Domnu asked, a trident in hand.

"I...I don't know." Raven didn't want to reveal the knife still tucked at her waistband. She was handy with a knife, but would a sword serve her better? She'd had some basic training in how to wield swords from her jiujitsu instructor, but otherwise that was it when it came to weapons. "I've never gone to battle before."

"Is that right? Didn't you kill a few of my men not too long ago?" Domnu's eyes sharpened as she walked over to her daughter. Leaning forward, she traced an icy finger across Raven's cheek. "Did you think that I wasn't watching, Raven? That I wouldn't know you were killing my people?"

"How was I supposed to know who they were? I just knew they were trying to hurt me," Raven retorted, reverting to her stubborn teenager act.

"That's fair, I suppose." Domnu thought about it and stepped back. "You fought well for not having gone to battle before."

"I lived on the streets. Every day was a battle."

"This will suit you. In fact, it might even be yours." Domnu reached for a gold blade on the wall, caught somewhere between a dagger and a sword, with delicate etching on the handle. "That's right, it belonged to your father now that I think about it."

"You...you took his blade after you killed him?" A note of incredulity filled Raven's voice as Domnu handed her the blade. Immediately, the sword hummed happily in Raven's hand, as though it had found its home, and Raven gaped down at the weapon. It felt almost warm to the touch, and a soothing current of liquid light poured from its handle and into her body, illuminating her soul.

It was love, she realized.

A magickal form of it, but in some way, her father was connecting with her through this blade.

And she knew, with certainty, that she now had the power to kill the Dark Goddess and rid the world of her terror forever.

"*Of course* I took the blade," Domnu said from across the room where she'd flung a door open. "No sense in wasting a well-crafted weapon. Come on, darling, let's go play, shall we? Oh, this is going to be fun. Mother and daughter's first battle together. Not the last of them, either, I hope." A delighted smile shone on Domnu's face, and her hair snarled around her, the snakes energized by her excitement. It was then that Raven read the madness in her eyes and fully understood that if she didn't stop Domnu, nobody ever would.

"Oh look, our toys have arrived." Domnu laughed as she stepped onto the flat roof that ran the length of one half of the castle, a low wall surrounding it. On one end, Kellen, Bianca, Seamus, Lily, and Callum stood, their Alicorns hovering in the air behind them. Raven's heart twisted at the sight of them, and she averted her eyes or she was going to start crying. Timing was everything now, and if Domnu suspected she would run back to Kellen, then she'd be dead before her sword dropped to the ground.

"I didn't think they'd come," Raven bit out, keeping her eyes on Domnu. It was the only place she could look without revealing her emotions, and she mustered all of her years of pretending like nothing bothered her and slipped an indifferent mask across her face. "Not the brightest, are they?"

"Raven. Just stop it. You don't have to do this," Kellen shouted, but Raven ignored him. Why wouldn't he just shut up? Didn't he know that he was only going to make this worse. "I love you, Raven. I love you. Come back to me."

"Awww, well, now. Isn't that just the sweetest thing in the world?" Domnu laughed and snapped her fingers, and Kellen dropped to his knees, grunting in pain. Unseen forces dragged him across the stone floor, until he was deposited in a lump in front of them. Quickly he stumbled to his feet, righting himself, and glared at

Domnu. "If you love my daughter then you need to ask for her hand in marriage."

"I will not," Kellen said, his chin lifting, "if marriage means that I side with you."

"A weak man. Unworthy of you," Domnu said, turning to study Raven's expression at the same time as she sliced her trident across Kellen's chest, instantly opening his skin so blood bloomed through his shirt, and he slumped once more to the ground. "We'll take extra time with destroying him, shall we? It will be our little fun, together."

"Yes, so much fun," Raven bit out over the bile that rose in her throat. Below them, screams sounded, and a roar came from the crowd. A soft thundering sound drifted from the murky green sky above them and Raven followed Domnu's eyes up.

"No," Domnu gasped, fury racing across her face, as hundreds of ravens descended upon her, pecking at her snakes and her eyes, and Domnu shrieked, throwing up her hands.

The sword heated in her hand, urging her on, and Raven understood that this was her moment. The only one she might get. Heart hammering, she took a deep breath, and opened her mouth in song.

"When she sings, queens will fall, daughters of blood, end them all."

Anger coated Domnu's face as the birds parted for Raven, and time seemed to slow, as she strode forward. Though her hand trembled on the sword, she lifted it.

"Daughter. You don't have it in you." Domnu's laugh was a harsh slap across Raven's soul.

"*Don't* I? Maybe it's just as easy as you abandoning me as a baby. Leaving me on the streets with nothing to protect me." Raven darted forward, neatly slicing the head from a lock of Domnu's hair, and the snakes screamed as one.

"It was for the best." Domnu's voice went soft, cajoling, and for once, Raven fully understood her own power.

"Or maybe it will be as easy as you killing my father after you used him for his seed."

Slice. Another snake went flying, its friends shrieking in distress.

"I was right to get rid of you." Domnu tilted her head and spat at Raven, her saliva landing on Raven's arm and burning like acid. Despite the pain, Raven refused to look away from the tragedy that was her mother.

"Just as I will be right to rid the world of the likes of you."

Leaping forward, Raven swung the sword, slicing neatly through her mother's neck, toppling her head from her body. Domnu's face was caught in a silent scream of rage, the snakes' fangs bared, before it dropped to the ground and rolled away. Her body instantly dissolved into a silvery puddle of blood, but the head lingered as her snakes blasted from her scalp, slithering away as fast as they could. The ravens swooped in, picking at the snakes like a team of school kids at a free pizza buffet, and Raven turned to run to Kellen.

Pain speared her calf.

Raven looked down to see a snake, its fangs imbedded in her calf, its eyes glowing as it sunk its deadly poison into her blood. Without a thought, she severed its head with the blade and ripped it from her skin, but already the poison seeped through her, icy darkness creeping up her limbs. Collapsing to the ground in front of where Kellen was pulling himself to his feet, she met his eyes.

"Raven, no. What's happened?" Kellen gasped out, fear on his handsome face.

"Snake," Raven gasped out. Kellen knelt by her side, his blood dripping onto her chest, and she reached up to run a hand across his cheeks, forcing him to look at her.

"Kellen."

"Shh, don't speak. We'll get you help. Raven, you didn't have to do this. We were here."

"I did, Kellen. *Kellen*," Raven yelled so he would stop babbling and look at her. When he did, she smiled. "I did this for you. I love you, Kellen, mighty ruler of the Air Fae. And I claim you back. Now, forever, and for all of time."

Light flashed, and a soft roaring filled her ears, as Kellen lifted her in the air, the world careening around her.

The last thing she saw was Riker bumping his head against hers, an image of a waterfall filling her mind, before a grey cloud drifted in front of her eyes, and she knew nothing more.

23

Kellen

Kellen cradled Raven in his arms, his own strength seeping from the wounds at his chest, while Riker carried them away from the Dark Realm. Below them, the world was shattering, like a dog ripping a toy apart at the seams, and the Domnua were falling through the cracks into nothingness as the world imploded without the Dark Goddess to lead it.

"Get the others out!" Kellen shouted.

"Just take her to safety. I've got this handled," Callum promised, and turned, diving on his Alicorn, Lily tucked safely in front of him.

Kellen urged Riker on, knowing they needed to be away from the Dark Magick that still lingered in this realm, but not certain where to take Raven. His own thoughts were growing murky with pain and whatever poison had been on Domnu's weapon. A blur of movement caught his eye, and then a small group of ravens converged in front of him, and he realized they were leading him.

"Go on, Riker. Follow them."

With that, Kellen closed his eyes and held on, bowing his head to whisper nonsense words of love against Raven's cold brow, praying that her heart still beat. Never had he seen such a stunning display of power as when daughter had stepped to mother, a song at her lips, a blade in hand. The courage Raven had shown was unlike any other he'd known, and he would worship her for all his days if he could only save her.

Riker let out a soft sound, a gentle warning, before his hooves touched the ground on landing. Kellen opened his eyes and looked around, unsure of where they'd landed. The ravens soared in circles around their heads, the sound of water at his back. Riker knelt, seeming to understand just how injured Kellen was, and Kellen slid from his back with Raven in his arms into the soft, damp sand.

They were at a beach.

Towering cliffs hugged the beach, cocooning them in an almost perfect C shape, and the ocean lapped softly against the sand. Kellen laid Raven down and pressed his fingers to her neck. The faintest of flutters met his fingers, and hope rippled through him. She wasn't gone yet.

"Riker. Where are we? What can I do?" Healing had never been one of the magicks he had strength in, and he couldn't understand why Riker and the ravens had brought him here, to an isolated beach, with nobody to help them. His strength waned, and he closed his eyes, forcing himself to breathe through the pain. "Riker, please go for help. We need to..."

A soft bark jolted him, and Kellen opened his eyes to see a dog, of all things, racing across the beach. The light shone faintly through the dog, and Kellen realized it was an apparition. Behind him, a woman hurried forward.

"I came as fast as I could." The woman held the same faint glow as the dog, and Kellen realized she was also of another realm. "Hi, I'm Fiona, and I'll be your healer today."

"It's..." Kellen rasped out the words, his energy sapping. "Fae magick. Dark magick. Domnu."

"Nasty woman." Fiona clucked her tongue and crouched by Raven. Her white hair hung in a cloud around her head and an amethyst necklace hung at her neck. She pulled out a pouch and sorted through it, before glancing back at Kellen with kind eyes. "What am I dealing with here?"

"Snake bite. Calf. Domnu's snakes."

"Oh." Fiona sat back on her heels, concern etched on her face. "I may need backup for this one. Are you safe here? Is Domnu after you?"

"No." Kellen shook his head, reaching out to thread Raven's fingers through his. "Dead. She's dead. Raven killed her."

"Killed...a goddess?" Happiness bloomed, and Fiona shot a hand in the air. "Let me...just...one second."

Fiona winked from sight, but her ghost puppy remained, running up to dance around Riker's legs. Riker seemed somewhat amused by the little guy and brought his head down to study it more closely.

"Riker."

Friend.

"You've been a good friend to me. My people. If I don't make it...please know how much I love you. You've brought me incredible joy through the years, my friend. You've been my companion, my sounding board, my shoulder to cry on. I'm forever grateful for what we have."

Turning, Kellen inched closer to Raven, needing to hold her close, as the poison worked its way through his system, dulling his thoughts and slowing his movements.

"My brave warrior. Forever on, and always, the warrior of my heart and soul. I came for you. I needed you to know that I would fight for you. And die for you. But never in vain my love, never. You did it. You did what nobody else could do, and the world will be a better place for it. My sweet nightbird. I'll love you always."

Something nudged Kellen, and he looked up to find Riker bent, his horn hovering near Kellen's forehead. Had the time come? Was Riker going to end it for him, so he didn't have to know the pain of death?

Riker touched his horn to Kellen's forehead.

A ripple of energy washed across his skin, and the image of the waterfall came to his head again, but this time it was Riker's magick pouring into him from his horn, chasing the toxic poison from his body. Kellen could feel it literally destroying the dark magick as his soul was pulled back into his body and the poison spit out into the night. Kellen gasped, jolting up like someone had just shocked him with a lightning bolt, and stared at Riker.

"You healed me. I didn't even know you could do that."

Friend.

At that moment, a glimmer of light appeared, and Riker dropped to his two front knees, bowing. Shocked, Kellen turned.

Fiona was back, but this time, the Goddess Danu accompanied her.

Kellen dropped to his knees as well.

He'd only ever seen the goddess once, when he was quite young, but his childhood memory of her held up. She was all that was light and good in the world, ethereal and flowing and glowing and lovely, and still she paled in comparison to the love of his heart, Raven.

"I'm sorry." Danu hurried forward, surprising Kellen by dropping to her knees next to Raven. "I was helping the others escape the Dark Realm. It's...no longer. It's gone. Without Domnu, it was but a house of cards." Danu lifted a hand and placed it at Raven's chest, whispering a few soft words. "The poison is strong, I fear. Domnu was particularly proud of her hair, but also quite crafty with her magicks. Her snake bites are the deadliest of her powers, and frankly, I'm surprised Raven has held on as long as she has."

A raven cawed above them, and Danu glanced up, a smile crossing her face.

"*Of course*, I'd forgotten. Do you know what your fated mate is?" Danu turned to Kellen who had inched forward on his knees so he could hold Raven's hand again. Why was she chatting so long? Shouldn't she be using all of her magick to heal Raven? Fury worked its way through him.

"She's about to be dead if you don't something."

"No, she's not," Danu quickly assured him, under-standing dawning. "Give her a moment to come to. She'll not die this night, I promise you that, Kellen of the Air Fae."

"She won't?" Kellen looked between Danu and Fiona who both wore happy smiles.

"Her father is an animal spirit. Of the birdsong people."

Kellen's mouth dropped open. There were lesser gods in the world, those that shifted between spirit and animal, and if Raven's father was one, then...she wasn't mortal at all.

"Raven," Kellen breathed, hope dancing through his chest. "My little nightbird. She's so, so tough. But her voice? Like music from the stars above."

"Yes, her voice is part of her magick." Danu beamed down at Raven when her eyelashes fluttered against her skin. "There she is. She'll be coming back to us now."

"I'm dead," Raven whispered, staring in awe at Danu, and the goddess laughed, a tinkle of windchimes in the breeze.

"No, not at all. You, my beautiful niece, are very much alive. Domnu's poison is almost gone now, but please, be careful with your movements."

"Kellen?" Raven asked, still blinking up at the goddess.

"I'm here. Right here, Raven. By your side. Always and forever," Kellen said, gripping her hand, and Raven slid her eyes to him without moving her face. A smile bloomed on her lips, and then she did the most heart-breaking thing of all.

She cried.

Tears poured from her, with such ferocity, that Kellen pulled her into his lap, cradling her close and rocked her, while she wept and wept against his chest. She cried the tears of someone who had once been lost, but now had found her way forward. Her body shook in his arms, and he murmured soft words in her ear, pressing his lips to her hair. Over her head, Riker stepped forward and bent his head to hers. At his soft whinny of concern, Raven looked up and gasped.

"Oh, Riker! You're safe. Oh, thank you. I was so worried. About everyone. I thought you all...I thought..." Raven looked up, her eyes stricken with guilt. "I didn't mean to hurt you but..."

"Shhh. We figured out pretty quickly what you were doing you stupid, stupid woman. Don't ever put yourself in danger like that again. I'd be furious with you if I wasn't so happy to see you alive," Kellen said, brushing his lips across hers in the softest of kisses. He was hungry for so much more, but now was certainly not the time.

"She's gone?" Raven asked, turning to look at Danu.

"She is." A mixture of relief and regret twisted across Danu's pretty face. "I'm certain of it."

"My mother. Your *sister*. I killed my mother." Tears filled Raven's eyes once again. "I'm sorry, Danu."

"Mother and sister in name only, my sweet niece. You have nothing to apologize for, Raven. You did what was right. What none of us could do ourselves, even me. Your mother made her own choices, and those decisions resulted in the end of her life. This is not on you to feel guilt for."

"Niece," Raven repeated, wiping the tears from her eyes. "I've never thought about having an aunt before."

"I think you have more family than you realize." Danu nodded to the birds that still swooped over their heads. "But that's a discussion for another time. I must go. There are rituals to be done now, to close off the Dark Realm. You'll be heavily rewarded for your help with this battle."

"I don't need anything." Raven turned and looked up at Kellen, with Riker standing over his shoulder. "I've got everything that I need."

With that, Danu winked from sight, and Fiona hovered nearby, her puppy running in circles at her feet.

"I just wanted to say that I'm sorry I had to leave you like that, but I wasn't sure I had enough power to heal Raven. Humans are one thing, but it's a bit over my head when it comes to the Fae and other gods." A light shone from the depths of the water, a brilliant blue, shimmering and shifting through the gently rolling waves. Fiona beamed. "Ah, look. That's my favorite thing to see."

"What is it?" Raven asked, her voice tinted with worry. Kellen tightened his arms around her, never wanting to let her go again.

"It's a story for another day." Fiona laughed. "But, welcome to Grace's Cove. Her waters are enchanted, and she shines in the presence of true love."

With that, Fiona turned and walked down the beach, the puppy at her feet, toward a man who waited by the cliff wall. They watched in silence as the waves lapped softly on the sand and the sea shone its light, until she reached the man and the three of them winked from sight.

Alone, and finally safe, Kellen helped Raven to her feet.

"So, you're sticking around, are you?" Raven looked at him as she dug in her jacket pocket.

"You can't get rid of me if you tried." Kellen laughed, love warming him.

"I'll hold you to that." Raven repeated his words from the moment they first met and flipped the amulet to him. Catching it in mid-air, Kellen grinned, knowing that finally, the Fae could live in peace.

EPILOGUE

THE SONG STARTED, low and tremulous, rippling across the clouds as the sun broke the horizon and kissed the sky with soft golden light. Hundreds of Alicorns flew, accompanied by the ravens, in perfect formation, as they gathered on the wind to celebrate and honor the life of Alistair, a fallen hero. All the Air Fae now knew that Alistair had rescued their treasured amulet from the clutches of Kellen's father who had planned to hand it to Domnu. In spite of his best efforts, he hadn't been able to return it to Kellen before their fateful last flight together.

Raven blinked at the tears that swam in her eyes at the sight. No, she hadn't known Alistair, but the grief on Kellen's face was tangible, and the beauty of the ceremony was enough to bring anyone to tears.

Or, perhaps, she'd learned that she was a crier.

Okay, that was a touch far. Raven reached down and stroked Riker's neck, having grown more confident with flying the Alicorns. Ever since she'd killed Domnu—she still couldn't refer to that woman as her mother—Raven had found that tears seemed to bubble up at the most inopportune times. Bianca had assured her that it likely came from years of repressing her emotions, but Raven wasn't quite certain she enjoyed it. She'd cried about a baby Alicorn tripping over its hooves the other day. The Alicorn had been fine, hopping right back up and racing around the field like a dog with the zoomies, but *still* Raven had shed a few tears. It was really getting out of hand.

The song grew in force, the melody rising on the wind, and Raven gasped as the riders released a shower of magick, droplets of gold, silver, and copper, until the clouds below them were coated in a shimmering blanket of magick. One by one, the Alicorns flew through the clouds, Alistair's name at their lips, a promise of memories never forgotten. The magick clung to their skin, coating them in a soft gleam, and once complete, they rose in one joyous formation, racing back to the castle. The ravens turned at the last moment, surrounding Raven with a flurry of acknowledgement, before careening off and returning to earth.

A few stayed with her.

It was something that Raven was still having to come to terms with, this whole daughter of spirits thing, but now as she thought back over her life, she realized just how often the ravens had come to watch over her. She'd always thought they were just birds with keen intelligence who were interested in the childish songs she'd sing by the river. She'd never had much food to share with them, but she'd always shared when she could. Only now, when she looked back, did she realize they'd often brought her gifts more than she'd ever given things to them. Sometimes it had been money, or a small trinket, or even food of their own they'd found. Even on her worst days, she'd never been alone, and Raven now hugged that knowledge to her heart.

Though both her parents were gone, Raven didn't grieve. How could she? They'd been gone her whole life, so losing them at this stage didn't much matter to her. Though a part of her was still interested in learning more about her father and his people. It was enough to have had a small understanding that the Fae existed through her life, but to learn about gods that shifted into animal form? Well, that was a whole new thing. Bianca had promised Raven that she would bring her loads of books on the subject matter, and Raven didn't doubt it.

As the Alicorns touched down at the castle, Raven turned to look at where Kellen sat on his, hugging his steed's neck, his face ravaged by grief.

A waterfall image popped in her head.

"Good call." Raven patted Riker's neck and nudged him toward Kellen.

"Kellen, will you come with me?" Raven asked, Riker already lifting back off the ground. Kellen's Alicorn followed suit automatically, as Raven had come to learn that Riker held some sort of rank in the Alicorn world.

"Of course, nightbird. Whatever you need." That was Kellen's nature, Raven had learned. It didn't matter if he was dealing with his own personal issues, he was always putting others first. Even when he was the one grieving, he immediately attended to her needs. It just made her love him all that much more.

Love.

Her stomach still twisted at how close she'd come to losing it all, particularly this feeling that now nestled happily in her heart. She'd heard of love through the years, hell, she'd even sung songs about it. But nothing came close to the way she felt when she was with Kellen. It was almost like the first time she'd closed the door to her very own flat, locking it behind her, and realized she could finally rest in safety. Kellen was home now, and with him, she felt safe.

"Where are you taking me?" Kellen asked, but then understanding dawned on his face as Riker flew toward a small forest that hugged the hillside, jagged mountain peaks rising into the air above. "Ah, Riker. My oldest friend. You're taking me to your favorite place, aren't you?"

Riker let out a happy hum of excitement, the sound rumbling through his body, and Raven couldn't wait to finally see this waterfall that Riker loved so dearly. They touched down on a grassy knoll next to a still pool of aquamarine water, and Raven slid to the ground, her mouth falling open in disbelief. Never had she seen something so magickal before, and she'd certainly seen her fair share of magickal things since she'd arrived in the Fae realm. But this? This was beyond anything she could have imagined.

A thick canopy of trees surrounded the pool, with vines of glimmering gold intertwining the branches, creating a canopy of leaves that sparkled in the sunlight like the first mist of morning clinging to a blade of grass. A river tumbled down the mountainside, with every color of the rainbow intermingling in its waters, like the light hitting a mermaid's scales. The water careened off a sharp cliff, pouring down the side of the mountain in a glorious glittering fall of color, before fading into the pool of pearlescent aquamarine. The sun warmed Raven's skin, and she wondered if she could entice Kellen in for a swim. Granted, she didn't know how to *actually* swim, but maybe they could just wade in the water. It was too magickal a place not to dip her toes in, right?

Kellen stood at her side, his arms outreached, and she willingly slid into them, taking the moment to lean into him. He'd lost both of his parents as well, even though his father still lived, and they both understood just how important it was to treasure those you loved.

"Of course, Riker. Go on, enjoy yourself. Thank you for bringing me here. It's exactly what I needed." Kellen's words rumbled at her ear as Raven pressed her head to his chest, and they stood like that for a moment longer, the tension of the day easing from their shoulders. Finally, Raven tilted her head and looked up at him.

"That was really lovely. The service. What an honor for Alistair and his family. I'm so glad that we learned what we did about him. You don't have to live with the thought that he'd betrayed you."

"Yes, one betrayal is more than enough." A grimace of pain crossed Kellen's face, and Raven tightened her arms around him.

Kellen's father had been sent away to wherever they put the bad people in the Fae realm. From Raven's understanding, that was with Callum at the Danula castle, where the high-ranking Fae had a magickal prison of sorts to house the people who had wronged the others. Exile had been presented as another option, but Kellen hadn't trusted that his father wouldn't harm others in the Earthly realm, so they'd agreed upon prison.

He hadn't spoken to his father before he'd been taken away. Raven had urged him to do so, hoping it would give him closure, but Kellen had assured her that his fist to his father's face had been all the closure he'd needed. It was tough to argue with that sentiment, seeing as how she'd decapitated her own mother, so Raven had let it go.

"Look." Kellen shifted, turning so Raven could view the waterfall, and her mouth dropped open.

At the top, Riker jumped, diving into the pool far below, and came up from the depths with a majestic flutter of his wings, sending a rainbow of droplets across the surface. Kellen's Alicorn followed suit, and soon the two raced back to the top, repeating the jump, before flying in and out of the sparkling fall of water. It reminded Raven of the baby Alicorn racing around the field trying to work off all the excited energy in its chubby, little body.

"I've never seen Riker like this," Raven exclaimed. "He's like a kid at a playground."

"It's the only place he really gets to let down his guard," Kellen explained, reaching for Raven's hand to tug her closer to the edge of the pool. "The other Alicorns look to him to lead, so he needs to be aware at all times. But here? Here is a protected space. He can be free to play."

"I love it," Raven breathed, laughter bubbling through her as the Alicorns chased each other in the sky. "He's so happy."

"It's his favorite place. And it also means he loves you because he brought you here."

"Really?" Raven whispered. Riker seemed to understand what they were talking about and flew down to them, landing a few feet away before plodding closer. His coat shone with droplets of water, turning him pearlescent in the sunlight, and Raven reached up to stroke his neck. "Just look at you, Riker. You positively glitter up here, don't you?"

Riker tossed his head, preening at her words.

"I love you, Riker," Raven said. "Thank you for bringing us here."

Riker nudged her with his nose, blowing a soft breath across her face, before turning to race into the sky once more.

"Do you want to go for a swim now that we're here? The water is refreshing. It can be both warm and cold, depending on what your body craves."

"Really? That's incredible," Raven said, tilting her head to study the shimmering water. She shouldn't be surprised at the magick that the Fae realm held, but sometimes the smallest of details, like water adjusting to the temperature you like, reminded her just how intricate Fae magick was. "I'd love to go in...but I can't swim. I was never taught how to."

"I'll keep you safe," Kellen promised.

His words settled into her, a soft sigh of acceptance, and soon they were stepping naked into the water. Much like Kellen had promised, the water was exactly the temperature that Raven had hoped it would be—like a hot spring of sorts—and she sighed happily as it enveloped her.

"Come here," Kellen said, pulling her so that her back rested against his chest, and he settled them into a comfortable seated position where the water lapped at their shoulders. "How do you find the water?"

"This is great. Like, really great. I've had enough of cold damp nights. But this? I could get used to this. It's really soothing, isn't it?"

"It is. I, too, went for warmth this time around. Some days, I enjoy nothing more than jumping into icy water. The shock to your body is quite invigorating. You jump out and wonder why you've made that choice, but once your blood is pumping, you realize how good it feels. Alistair and I used to come here to play as boys. The Alicorns would look after us. I think he'd be happy we are here right now." Kellen's arms tightened around Raven, and she let the silence surround them, understanding that there wasn't much to be said in this moment. Healing took its own time, and they both would find their way, together.

A thought popped in her head, something that had been bothering her for weeks now, and she shifted as she tried to determine if now would be an appropriate time to bring it up.

"Just say it, Raven." Kellen's voice laughed at her ear. He always seemed to know when she was battling with her thoughts.

"Remember how I told you about this youth group that I worked with?"

"I do, yes."

"There's this girl there. Taryn. She doesn't really have anyone, and I promised that I would come back to her...and..."

"You want to bring her here?" Kellen asked, and Raven twisted to look up at him, excitement dancing through her.

"Can I? I mean only, of course, if she wants to come. I thought maybe to just visit her and let her know that I was safe and still thinking about her. But if I could bring her here? I mean, that's a huge undertaking, Kellen. She's only twelve or so. She's a child. She'll need help and..."

"We can adopt her."

"What?" Raven gasped, pressing her hands to Kellen's chest, hope blooming in her heart. "You'd...but...we haven't..."

"Talked about children? Yes, I want them. I want a life with you, Raven. I want to build a home, a family, a future with you. You're *my* fated mate. Whatever you want, I want."

"I...but..." Raven blinked at him. "I never considered being a mother. It was never in my future. I didn't even—"

"Isn't that what you've been doing all along? Mothering this Taryn?"

"I, well, I guess, maybe?" Raven bit her lip as she considered. "I don't know. She just worked her way in. She's a good kid, Kellen. She's been dealt a bad hand, has her walls up, but she has nobody. We could give her a future plucked right out of a fairy tale."

"Then we should. If it's what you want. If you love her, then I will too." Kellen rose, pulling Raven to stand with him, and she gaped at him as water ran in rivulets down his naked body. Distracted for a moment, just by his sheer beauty and the splendor of their surroundings, she lost the thread of the conversation. A knowing smile slipped across Kellen's lips, and he bent over to brush his lips gently across hers.

"That's for later, little nightbird. Let's go rescue your girl."

"Oh, this is so exciting. How will we do it?" Raven clapped her hands, accepting the towel that Kellen gave her. Much like any Fae magick, they were dry in moments and dressed, and Riker flew to meet them.

"What will make the most sense to your friend? We don't want to scare her."

"There's not much that scares her, but I'm sure she'll be overwhelmed." Raven tapped her finger against her lips as she thought about it. "I think we need to go back, but I need to approach her alone before you reveal yourselves. And I think the Alicorns need to be there. I don't know any kid that would turn down a chance to ride on an Alicorn."

"Then we go. We find your friend, and Riker and I will conceal ourselves until you are ready for us. The ravens will come with us as well." Kellen smiled down at her, and traced a finger over her cheek as she looked up at him in awe.

"I don't know what to say. You have no idea what this

will mean to her. What it could have meant to me as a child if I'd had someone rescue me."

"But you rescued yourself, didn't you, nightbird?"

Raven's heart split open with love for this impossibly good man, and before she knew it, they were hurtling toward Galway, the wind blowing her hair back, her mission filling her with excitement.

They touched down in the empty alleyway behind the Youth Center, a few birds circling their heads, and Raven slipped from Riker's back.

"You'll be safe?" Raven looked up at Kellen, worry on her face.

"Nobody will know we're here. Go get our girl," Kellen said, and Raven's heart filled.

Turning, she raced down the alleyway and around the corner, knowing that the center would be open soon. Typically, a few of the kids would mill about in the area, and if she was lucky, she'd be able to catch Taryn on the street. Sure enough, Raven caught a glimpse of a tangle of blonde hair and a thin flannel jacket in a muted purple that Taryn always wore.

"Pssst. Taryn," Raven whispered, and Taryn, as attuned to the streets as Raven was, whirled at the sound. Her eyes widened at the sight of Raven, but Raven held a finger to her lips before the girl could say anything. Beckoning with her hand, she ducked around the corner of the building, hoping Taryn would follow. When she did, Raven turned and squatted at Taryn's feet.

"You came back," Taryn whispered. The happiness on her face was replaced quickly with suspicion. Raven couldn't blame her. She was acting odd, and Taryn would pick up on any nuance in her tone. "I didn't think you would."

"I promised you, didn't I? Fringe friends forever." Raven glanced around, making sure they were still alone. "Listen..."

"Where were you? You've been gone, like, a month at least. I didn't think you were coming back." Taryn picked at a hole in her jacket, pretending nonchalance.

"I've always said that I would come back to you, Taryn. I don't lie to my friends, do I?"

When Taryn shrugged one shoulder, Raven continued. "I don't know if you'll believe me if I tell you. But I can *show* you where I've been. The thing is...I have a really, really, big secret. And I want to share it with you."

"A secret? I like secrets." Interest bloomed in Taryn's dirty face.

"I do too. See, sharing a secret means we trust each other. And I'm going to trust you with something really magickal, Taryn. Because I want to also ask you something." Raven reached out, keeping her hand in the air in front of Taryn, allowing the girl the choice if she wanted to take Raven's hand or not.

"What is it?" Taryn waited.

"I want you to come with me, Taryn. I want to take you away from all of this and give you the life you *should* be living."

Hope bloomed instantly in Taryn's eyes, but quickly it was shuttered.

"Yeah, I've heard that before." Taryn kicked a pebble on the street in front of her. Still Raven kept her hand outstretched.

"Me too. I heard it dozens of times until I stopped believing. But I'm asking you to take a chance, Taryn. On me. On us. I want you to be a part of my family. I've come back, just for you, and then we're leaving Galway forever. If you'll be a part of my family, that is..."

"You're...wait, what? You want to, like, adopt me?" Taryn squinted at her. "For real?"

"For real and forever. If you'll have me. But..." Raven lifted a finger before Taryn could respond. "You need to know all the facts first. That's not my secret. Remember when I was running from trouble?"

"Yes." It was a whisper, and Taryn watched her with suspicious eyes.

"I was dealing with some magickal bad guys. The Fae to be exact." Raven waited while Taryn rolled her eyes. "I know. Trust me, sure and I know it's sounding ridiculous. But it's the truth. The Fae are real, and if you come with me, you never have to live here again. You can come to a magickal world and live as a fairy princess."

"Now you're just taking the piss out of me," Taryn grumbled, anger flashing across her face. "I thought you really wanted to see me."

"I'm not, I promise. Just..." Raven turned her head. "Kellen? Can you come here?"

In seconds, Kellen appeared at their side with the two Alicorns and a soft wheezing sound escaped Taryn. The girl instantly gripped Raven's hand, leaning into her side, as she gaped up at the Alicorns in shock.

"I guess it is easier to show you, isn't it?"

"Are those real?" Taryn whispered in Raven's ear.

"They are. Pretty cool, huh? And this man right here?

That's Kellen. He's my...well, he's my everything. We want you to be a part of our family, if you are okay with leaving Galway and coming to live with us."

"Where?" Taryn asked.

"With the Fae. In another land."

"Will they be there?" Taryn pointed at the Alicorns.

"Loads of them. Babies even. You can learn to fly them. What do you say?" Raven turned to face Taryn, hope dancing in her chest.

"You've never lied to me. Not once," Taryn said, meeting Raven's eyes. "Adults always lie to me. Or tell me, like, half the truth. Except you. You said it like it was. Even when it was hard to hear. You didn't treat me like I was stupid or annoying."

"You're not stupid or annoying. You've always been my favorite, Taryn. You've got a good heart, and I know how much you hate being on the street. You're not like the others. Remember how you returned that woman's phone? The street hasn't broken you. This is your chance to live a life beyond your wildest dreams. Please, let me give you this, a home, a family, magick, even."

"And him?" Taryn shifted, glancing up at where Kellen smiled down from his Alicorn. "He's not gonna hurt me?"

"Oh, Taryn. No, *never*. He's not like that. And even if someone tried, the Alicorns will have your back. They are fiercely protective of their young."

"They'd protect me?" Taryn's eyes widened, and Raven wondered if Riker was projecting an image in her head.

"They would. So, what do you say? Will you be my

family, Taryn?" This time, Raven stood and held out her hand, waiting. When Taryn finally reached out, her small palm gripping Raven's tightly, Raven's heart broke open.

"Fringe friend forever," Taryn said.

"Fringe *family* forever," Raven amended, her heart brimming with happiness as they took flight, leaving the streets of Galway behind forever.

I hope my books have added a little magick into your life. If you have a moment to add some to my day, you can help by telling your friends and leaving a review. Word-of-mouth is the most powerful way to share my stories. Thank you.

Read on for a taste of Wild Scottish Knight, Book One in the Wall Street Journal bestselling Enchanted Highlands series.

AUTHOR'S NOTE

There's a part of me that is always sad when I bring a series to a close, and this time is no different. When I first started writing the Wildsong series, having introduced you to Lily and Callum in Wild Irish Christmas, I had no idea the journey it would take me on. And, let me tell you, this last book hit me in all the feels. While I was far too young to ever remember my time in a foster home, as an adopted child with a familial relationship that is best defined as – "It's complicated" – Raven's story resonates with me. I, too, have often found myself on the outside looking in, sighing over what-if's and lost chances for connection. That being said, I still believe we get to be the heroine of our own story, and I apply that mantra to my daily life. Thank you for coming on this journey with me, my sparkly amazing readers! I know I often take you on some wild swings of emotion from joy to tears and back again, but that's what life is all about, isn't it?

As always, a huge thank you to my soulmate, the Scotsman. He's my steady foundation, the ultimate hype man, and I'm lucky to have someone who champions me the way that he does. Thank you to the Scotsman's family for everything from helping to shine up the story to giving feedback on cover designs. I've kind of dragged my in-laws into the publishing industry with me, and I'm lucky to have them along for the ride.

And last, but never least, a thousand kisses to my sweet dog, Blue, who is glued to my side as I write this.

Sparkle on!

Tricia O'Malley

If you missed Wild Irish Christmas you can join my newsletter and as a welcome gift, I will send you a digital copy of Wild Irish Christmas right to your inbox. Use the link or scan the QR code to get your copy today.

https://offer.triciaomalley.com/free

WILD SCOTTISH KNIGHT

SOPHIE

WHAT WAS it about death that brought out the worst in people? Most of those in attendance at the celebration of life event today hadn't spoken to my uncle in years, and now I was being showered with rabid curiosity dressed up as forced condolences. Let's be honest. Uncle Arthur had been filthy rich, and everybody was here for the READING OF THE WILL. Yes, I heard it like that in all caps whenever someone asked me about the READING OF THE WILL. I barely suppressed a hysterical giggle as I envisioned a small man with a heralding trumpet, standing on the balcony and unfurling a long roll of paper, reading off the terms of THE WILL like Oprah during her Christmas specials. *And you get a car...and you get a boat...*

I was currently winning the bet on how many times

my uncle's ex-wives would try to console me, a fact which simultaneously cheered and annoyed me. There were seven wives in total, having multiplied like Gremlins being exposed to water, before his last, and my favorite, had cured my uncle of his marrying hastily habit.

Bagpipes sounded behind me, and though I wasn't usually a nervous sort, my drink went flying. Turning, I glared at the bagpiper who had the gall to wink at me. Cheeky bastard, I thought, narrowing my eyes as he confidently strode past, parting the crowd like a hot knife through butter. Suitably impressed, because the bagpipe was the type of instrument that demanded attention, my eyes followed the man as he crossed the lawn, kilt billowing in the wind.

"Dammit, Sophie." Wife Number Two glared at me and dabbed at her tweed jacket in sharp motions. "This is Chanel." The only thing tighter than the woman's severe bun was her grasp on my uncle's alimony. Before I could apologize, Number Two strode off, snapping her finger at a caterer, her lips no doubt pursed in disapproval. Only my uncle would plan and cater his own funeral. I grabbed another glass of champagne from the tray of a passing server.

Arthur MacKnight of Knight's Protective Services, leader in home and commercial security systems world-wide, did not leave anything to chance. His attention to detail, pragmatic attitude, and strong code of ethics had rocketed his company to the top of the list. On the personal side? Arthur had been a known eccentric, disgustingly wealthy, and one of my favorite people. With a ten-figure company on the line, I guess I couldn't blame people for wanting to know the contents of THE WILL. But not me. I didn't care about the money. I just wanted my uncle back.

"Prissy old scarecrow," Lottie MacKnight whispered in my ear. As the proud owner of the title of Wife Number Seven, Lottie had withstood the test of time and had made Arthur very happy in his later years. She was creative, quirky, and the most down to earth of all the wives, and I had bonded with her instantly over our shared hatred of fancy restaurants. I still remembered giggling over a plate that had been delivered with much finesse but carried little more than a sliver of carrot with a puff of foam. Arthur had looked on, amusement dancing in his eyes, as his new wife and only niece had tried to maintain their composure in front of the stuffy maître d'.

When I was twelve, I had come home one day to the contents of my bedroom being placed in boxes by our very apologetic housekeeper. Much to my horror, my parents had informed me—via a note on the kitchen counter, mind you—that I was leaving for boarding school that same evening. Somehow, Lottie had caught wind of it and rescued me, bringing me back home to live with her and Arthur. I'd happily settled into a life of contradictions—business lessons at breakfast, fencing lessons at lunch, and magick studies after dinner. Well, not magick per se, but Arthur had nourished an insatiable love for myths, legends, and the unexplainable.

Once a year, I dutifully endured a phone call with my parents from whatever far-flung destination they were visiting. As an afterthought, I would occasionally receive inappropriate birthday gifts that would leave me blinking in confusion. A few we kept for the sheer madness of it all, like the gold-plated two-foot penguin statue. Lottie had promptly named it Mooshy, set him in the front hall, and put little hats or bows on him, depending on the occasion. Because of them, my tender teenage years had gone from stilted and awkward to vibrant and fulfilled, and I would forever be grateful.

Arthur's loss numbed me, like someone had cut out the part of me where my feelings were supposed to reside, and now I was just shambling about making awkward small talk with people who were suddenly very interested in speaking with me. Even the Old Wives Club, as Lottie and I referred to the other six wives, had made weak attempts at mothering me. Hence the bet I'd made with Lottie. Upon arrival at the funeral, the wives had besieged me, like a murder of crows dressed in couture, angry in the way of perpetually hungry people. Lottie, being Lottie, had swooped forward in her colorful caftan and flower fascinator, rescuing me from the wives by cheerfully suggesting they look for the attorney who carried THE WILL. The Old Wives Club had pivoted as one, like a squadron of fighter planes, and narrowed in on the beleaguered attorney with ruthless efficiency.

The funeral was being held on the back lawn of Arthur's estate in California, his castle towering over the proceedings. Yes, *castle*. Arthur had built his house to remind him of the castles in Scotland, much to the chagrin of the neighborhood. His neighbors, their houses all sleek lines and modern angles, had hated Arthur's castle. I *loved* it. What was the point of earning all that

money if you couldn't have fun with it? Arthur had nourished a deep affection for his Scottish roots, often trav-
eling there several times a year, and had spent many a
night trying to convince me to enjoy what he claimed
were the finest of Scottish whiskies. As far as I was
concerned, if that was the best Scotland could do, then I
was not impressed.

It was one of those perpetually cheerful California
days, and the sun threatened to burn my fair skin. Arthur
had always joked that he could get a sunburn walking to
the mailbox and back. He wasn't far off. I'd already
wished I had brought a hat with me. Instead, I slid my
bargain-bin sunglasses on my nose to dull the light.
Designer sunglasses were a no-go for me. At the rate I sat
on my sunglasses and broke them, it was far more
economical for me to grab some from the rack on the way
out of the gas station.

"Nice glasses. Dior?" Wife Number Three drifted up,
her knuckles tight on the martini glass she held.

"No, um, BP." I nodded. I pronounced it as Bay-Pay,
skewing the name of the gas station.

"Hmm, I haven't heard of them. I'll be sure to look for
their show this spring in Paris. Darlings!" Number Three
fluttered her fingers at a fancy couple and left to air-kiss
her way into an invitation to a yacht party.

"Break another pair of sunglasses?" Lottie asked,
biting into a cube of cheese. There was cheese? I looked
around for the server who carried that coveted tray and
grinned.

"Third this week."

"That's a lot for you." Lottie turned to me, her eyes

searching my face. "You okay, sweetie? This is a tough time for us. I loved Arthur, and I'll miss him like crazy, but it's different for you. He was like…"

"My father," I whispered, spying my own parents across the lawn, who had arrived over an hour ago and still hadn't bothered to greet their only daughter. Their indifference to my existence still shouldn't sting…*yet*. Here we were. I tried to frame it in my head like they were just people who I used to room with back in the day.

"And as your mother"—Lottie waved a jewel-encrusted hand at my parents—"I don't care that those two idiots are here. *I'm* claiming Mama rights. So as your stand-in mother, I want to make sure you'll be able to grieve properly. I'm here for you, you know."

"I know, I know." I pressed a kiss to Lottie's cheek, catching the faint scent of soap and turpentine. Lottie must have been painting her moods again. She was a world-renowned painter in her own right and worked through her emotions on her canvasses. All of Arthur's and my spreadsheets and business talk had made her eyes glaze over with boredom. "I don't really know yet how to think or feel. I'm numb, if I'm being honest."

"Numb is just fine. As Pink Floyd would attest to…it's a comfortable place to be. Just live in that space for a little bit, and we'll handle what comes. What about Chad? Or is it Chet?" Lottie affected a confused expression, though I knew very well she knew my boyfriend's name.

My boyfriend, Chad, was good-looking in a polished private school kind of way, and at first, I'd just been drawn to someone who'd paid careful attention to me. Now, as I watched him schmooze my parents—*not that he knew they were my parents*—I felt an odd sort of detachment from him. Perhaps that was grief numbing my feelings. Or maybe I liked the idea of a Chad more than an actual Chad himself.

"He's been very supportive," I told Lottie. Which was true. Chad had doted on me constantly since Arthur had died, but so had all my new besties who had crawled out of the woodwork upon the news of Arthur's death. Lottie patted my arm and turned as the celebrant began speaking.

The words flowed over me, intertwining and blurring together, as my own memories of Arthur flashed through my mind. Our heated fencing battles—a sport Arthur had insisted I learn—his quirky obsession with all things Scottish, his willingness to always listen to any new ideas I had for the company, and the way he'd always called me his wee lassie. No, I wasn't ready to say goodbye.

"Oh, shit." Lottie gripped my arm, her fingers digging into the soft flesh, and I pulled myself from my thoughts to see what had distracted Lottie.

The bagpiper had returned to the back of the crowd, having circled the lawn, and now stood waiting for the celebrant's signal. Behind him, Arthur's five Scottish Terriers tumbled about.

"Did you let the dogs out?" I whispered, horror filling me. Arthur's Scotty dogs, while decidedly adorable, were quite simply put—terrors.

"No, I didn't. But the lawyer had asked where they were..." Understanding dawned, and we turned to each other.

"Arthur," I said, shaking my head.

"That *crazy* man. God, I loved him." Lottie brushed at a tear as the wail of bagpipes began again, and the kilted man once more strode forward.

"*Amazing Grace.*" For one haunting moment, the music transported me to another time where I could just imagine a Scottish warrior crossing the land in search of his love. Romantic thoughts which had no place here, I reminded myself, fixated on the bagpiper. The dogs bounced after the man like he was a Scottish Pied Piper, and only then did I see that one of them carried a large stuffed Highland cow. *Coo*, I automatically corrected myself. A heiland coo had been one of Arthur's favorite things to photograph on his travels to Scotland, and he'd even talked of developing a Coo-finder app so that the tourists could more easily get their own photographs.

"You don't think..." A thought occurred to me, but it was so ridiculous I couldn't bring myself to say it.

"Nothing that man did surprised me." Lottie chuckled. We watched with horrified fascination as the dogs reached the front of the funeral gathering. The Old Wives Club shifted in unison, likely due to the possibility of getting dog hair on their Chanel, and I couldn't look away from the impending doom. It was like watching a couple fight in public—I knew it was bad to eavesdrop, but I always wanted to listen and pick whose side I was on. Spoiler alert. I usually sided with the woman.

"Tavish and Bruce always fight over toys," I hissed as two of the dogs separated themselves from the pack, their ears flattening.

"Arthur knows...*knew* that," Lottie said, her hand still gripping my arm. I winced as it tightened. A gasp escaped me when the dogs leapt at each other. Houston, we have a problem.

A flurry of barking exploded as the last notes of *"Amazing Grace"* faded into the sun, and the bagpiper strolled away seemingly unconcerned with the chaos he left in his wake. Maybe he was used to it, for the Scots *could* be unruly at times, and this was just another day's work for him. I grimaced as Tavish and Bruce got ahold of the coo, each gripping a leg, and pulled with all their might. The celebrant, uncertain what to do, walked forward and made shooing gestures with his hands.

The dogs ignored him, turning in a manic circle, whipping their heads back and forth as they enjoyed a fabulous game of tug. Growls and playful barks carried over the stunned silence of the gathering, with everyone at a loss of how to proceed.

With one giant rip, Bruce won the toy from Tavish and streaked through the horrified crowd. A fine white powder exploded from the coo, coating the Old Wives Club and spraying the front line.

"His ashes," I breathed. My heart skipped a beat.

"Indeed," Lottie murmured.

Bruce broke from the crowd and tore across the lawn toward the cliffs, the rest of the dogs in hot pursuit, a doggy version of Braveheart. Tavish threw his head back and howled, and I was certain I could just make out the cry for "freeeeedom" on the wind.

The wind that now carried a cloud of ashes back to the funeral gathering.

Pandemonium broke out as the crowd raced for the castle, trying to beat the ash cloud, while Lottie and I stood upwind to observe the chaos from afar. A muffled snort had me turning my head.

"You can't possibly be..." I trailed off as Lottie pressed her lips together in vain, another snort escaping. To my deep surprise, the numb space inside me unlocked long enough for amusement to trickle in. In moments, we were bent at the waist, howling with laughter, while the Old Wives Club shot us death glares from across the lawn.

"Oh." Lottie straightened and wiped tears from her eyes. "Arthur would've loved that."

I wrapped an arm around Lottie and watched Wife Number Three vomit into a bush.

"It's almost like he planned it." As soon as I said the words, I *knew* he had. Raising my champagne glass to the sky in acknowledgment, I felt the first bands of grief unknot inside me. He'd wanted us to laugh, as his last parting gift, to remember that in the face of it all...the ridiculous was worth celebrating.

Continue reading Wild Scottish Knight today!

ALSO BY TRICIA O'MALLEY

The Isle of Destiny Series

Stone Song

Sword Song

Spear Song

Sphere Song

A completed series in Kindle Unlimited.

Available in audio, e-book & paperback!

"Love this series. I will read this multiple times. Keeps you on the edge of your seat. It has action, excitement and romance all in one series."

- Amazon Review

The Enchanted Highlands

Wild Scottish Knight

Wild Scottish Love

A Kilt for Christmas

Wild Scottish Rose

"I love everything Tricia O'Malley has ever written and "Wild Scottish Knight" is no exception. The new setting for this magical journey is Scotland, the home of her new husband and soulmate. Tricia's love for her husband's country shows in every word she writes. I have always wanted to visit Scotland but have never had the time and money. Having read "Wild Scottish Knight" I feel I have begun to to experience Scotland in a way few see it. I am ready to go see Loren Brae, the castle and all its magical creatures, for myself. Tricia O'Malley makes the fantasy world of Loren Brae seem real enough to touch!"

-Amazon Review

Available in audio, e-book, hardback, paperback and is included in your Kindle Unlimited subscription.

The Wildsong Series

Song of the Fae

Melody of Flame

Chorus of Ashes

Lyric of Wind

"The magic of Fae is so believable. I read these books in one sitting and can't wait for the next one. These are books you will reread many times."

- Amazon Review

A completed series in Kindle Unlimited.

Available in audio, e-book & paperback!

The Siren Island Series

Good Girl

Up to No Good

A Good Chance

Good Moon Rising

Too Good to Be True

A Good Soul

In Good Time

A completed series in Kindle Unlimited.

Available in audio, e-book & paperback!

"Love her books and was excited for a totally new and different one! Once again, she did NOT disappoint! Magical in multiple ways and on multiple levels. Her writing style, while similar to that of Nora Roberts, kicks it up a notch!! I want to visit that island, stay in the B&B and meet the gals who run it! The characters are THAT real!!!" - Amazon Review

The Althea Rose Series

One Tequila

Tequila for Two

Tequila Will Kill Ya (Novella)

Three Tequilas

Tequila Shots & Valentine Knots (Novella)

Tequila Four

A Fifth of Tequila

A Sixer of Tequila

Seven Deadly Tequilas

Eight Ways to Tequila

Tequila for Christmas (Novella)

"Not my usual genre but couldn't resist the Florida Keys setting. I was hooked from the first page. A fun read with just the right amount of crazy! Will definitely follow this series."- Amazon Review

A completed series in Kindle Unlimited.

Available in audio, e-book & paperback!

The Mystic Cove Series

Wild Irish Heart

Wild Irish Eyes

Wild Irish Soul

Wild Irish Rebel

Wild Irish Roots: Margaret & Sean

Wild Irish Witch

Wild Irish Grace

Wild Irish Dreamer

Wild Irish Christmas (Novella)

Wild Irish Sage

Wild Irish Renegade

Wild Irish Moon

"I have read thousands of books and a fair percentage have been romances. Until I read Wild Irish Heart, I never had a book actually make me believe in love."- Amazon Review

A completed series in Kindle Unlimited.

Available in audio, e-book & paperback!

Stand Alone Novels

Ms. Bitch

"Ms. Bitch is sunshine in a book! An uplifting story of fighting your way through heartbreak and making your own version of happily-ever-after."

~Ann Charles, USA Today Bestselling Author

Starting Over Scottish

Grumpy. Meet Sunshine.

She's American. He's Scottish. She's looking for a fresh start. He's returning to rediscover his roots.

One Way Ticket

A funny and captivating beach read where booking a one-way ticket to paradise means starting over, letting go, and taking a chance on love...one more time

10 out of 10 - The BookLife Prize

CONTACT ME

Love books? What about fun giveaways? Nope? Okay, can I entice you with underwater photos and cute dogs? Let's stay friends, receive my emails and contact me by signing up at my website

www.triciaomalley.com

Or find me on Facebook and Instagram.
@triciaomalleyauthor

Printed in Great Britain
by Amazon